INFAMOUS LOVE

A BLACK LIGHT PREQUEL

LIVIA GRANT

Published by Black Collar Press

Editing by Paul Von Karmann

Cover Artist - Eris Adderly

Ebook ISBN: 978-0-9982191-0-3

This book is intended for adults only. Spanking and other sexual activities represented in this book are fantasies and intended for mature readers only. All characters are fictional.

First Electronic Edition: October, 2016

❀ Created with Vellum

BLACK LIGHT SERIES

For my "Sprint Girls". I'm so lucky to have you in my life to talk me off the ledge occasionally, and remind me every so often that this author gig is a marathon, not a sprint. Love you Jennifer, Sophie, Myra, Lee and Addison.

CHAPTER 1

EMMA'S JOURNEY

"*Y*ou seriously can't do this to me, Bianca. This is below low, even for you." Emma hated the hint of fear heard in her voice. She'd be damned if she was going to let her travel companion know how freaked out she was at the thought of making her way home by herself.

"I swear. You're acting as if you haven't lived here for the last semester. You've been to Paris twice with me. This should be a piece of cake for you by now." The mocking laughter thrown back in her face replaced Emma's fear with anger.

"You promised me. I told you from the beginning that I didn't speak any French. You swore you'd stick with me to help me travel!"

"You've been here for five months. I can't help it if you're incapable of learning a foreign language."

Emma took a deep breath and bit her tongue to keep from saying something she'd regret later. She should have known better than to trust Bianca to keep her word. She never had before, so why should today be different? Still, leaving your friend stranded in a foreign country where she didn't speak the language so you could run off for the weekend with a smooth talking Italian on a

1

motorcycle was low even for Bianca. Then again, they weren't really friends, were they?

Emma decided to change tactics. "What do you know about this guy? What's his name again? Mario?"

"You're saying it wrong. It's Marrrio" she whined, rolling the R.

"Whatever. What about Pieter? Just last week, you were ready to move to France forever to stay with him."

Her friend got a distasteful look on her face. "Yeah, well Pieter showed me his true colors. He came clean with his women's lingerie fetish when I caught him trying on my panties."

Having seen Pieter, this information did not come as a surprise to Emma. In fact, it made a lot of sense. "Fine. Then why not go home to John? I know he'd take you back in a heartbeat."

"John's a boy. I'm ready for a man."

Emma couldn't stop the snort. "No offense. I've seen Mario and if he's not careful, his motorcycle is going to crush him like a bug. He's pretty skinny for a *man*."

Bianca's patience was coming to an end. "Not all of him is skinny, if you get my drift." The sly smile that accompanied her raunchy innuendo painted Bianca as the slut that she was. In spite of having a decent boyfriend waiting for her back in Wisconsin, Bianca had used the five months they'd been studying abroad in France to 'sow her wild oats' as she'd described it. Loosely translated, that meant she had slept with no less than six guys, and those were just the ones Emma knew about.

Looking into Bianca's eyes, Emma knew she was about to be deserted in Nice, a quaint town along the Mediterranean. She had two days to make her way to Paris in time to take her flight from Paris' Charles de Gaulle airport back home to Madison.

"Listen, this hotel is nice. Why don't you stay here, ditch your flight and I'll have Mario bring me back here in a few days and we'll go home together then? He's gonna take me over to Florence for a bit of shopping, but...." Bianca cut off abruptly. For the first time in the entire conversation, she appeared guilty.

"Florence. Seriously? The city I begged you to go with me to last month and you told me was a waste of time? That Florence?" Emma's normally patient demeanor was crumbling. Anger she'd been pushing down for months started to bubble up. A feeling akin to an exploding volcano uncharacteristically erupted from her and she found herself near screaming in the middle of the upscale hotel lobby.

"You really are a slutty bitch, you know that? You have a wonderful boyfriend waiting for you at home, but you decide to sleep your way across the continent instead. You want to expose yourself to every STD, have at it, but I thought you at least had enough decency to keep your word to me. I told you I didn't speak French and I was coming here to teach classes in English. More importantly, you know damn well I can't stay here and wait for you while you fuck your way across Europe. Some of us don't have a rich daddy who'll buy us another first class ticket home - or who will pay for expensive hotels instead of youth hostels like normal backpacking students. No. Some of us actually have to get back because we have that four-letter word. J-O-B-S. You know I start my TA job next week. I need the money. I can't miss it. So you go off to spend daddy's money in the city I wanted to go to, while I figure out how the hell to get myself home. All I ask is you do me one final favor."

Bianca at least had the decency to keep her mouth shut while guiltily shuffling her sandal-covered feet. Emma was shaking with emotion. She'd never gone off on anyone as she just had. For once in her life, she had stood up for herself and it felt fucking fantastic.

Emma wasn't proud of herself, but she spat the hateful words anyway. "The second you get home, drop my class because I don't want to have to look out into the lecture hall and see you sitting there, knowing the only reason you're there is because you think I'll give you an easy A. You should stick with your original game plan of sleeping with your professors

LIVIA GRANT

for grades. That strategy appears to be working exceptionally well for you."

The surprise on Bianca's face as the insult hits home reminded Emma she was on new ground. She'd always been the steady friend. The brainiac, studious friend. The pretty, but plump friend. She despised being the friend who got to watch the purses back at the table while the sexy girls went out on the dance floor with the hot guys who asked them to dance.

Emma was sick of watching the purses.

Bianca reminded Emma that she had years of bitch practice on her. "You really are a cunt, Emma. I can't believe I thought you were my friend."

Emma counters, "Me? I'm not acting like a friend? Incredible. Your selfishness knows no bounds."

Bianca reached down to grab the handle of her expensive luggage, managing to get in the last word. "I was going to buy you a souvenir in Florence, but you can forget that now." And off she flounced towards the revolving front door where Mario with the rolling R waited holding a helmet. Emma smiled knowing how much Bianca would hate putting on the helmet because it would mash down the curls she had spent twenty minutes perfecting. She also wondered where Marrrio would strap Bianca's oversized suitcase.

Once the object of her anger was out of sight, the reality of her situation closed in on Emma. She moved the few feet to the seating area on the fringe of the hotel lobby, and sank into the soft leather couch.

She would have loved to panic, but she was too cool-headed. Traveling alone without speaking fluent French was going to be stressful, but she'd managed to pick up enough to get by. She also knew she would be able to find people who spoke English to help her if she got into real trouble. It was more the principle of being stranded thousands of miles from home that had Emma upset.

4

And that she continued to let shallow people like Bianca into her life.

She was about to stand to head to the elevator when two couples drew her attention as they approached. Emma sat back, trying to look casual as they strolled in her direction.

It didn't take long to figure out what had caught her eye. The couples were picture perfect. They looked as if they'd come from a photo shoot for the front of a *Lifestyles of the Rich and Famous* magazine.

The women were both outfitted from head to toe in high-end designer clothes and shoes. Emma was no expert, but she suspected their Gucci purses cost more than she made in a whole semester. The realization depressed her, and only intensified as she turned her attention to the men they were with. They could only be described as pure perfection.

While the women appeared snooty and arrogant, the men appeared down-to-earth in their khaki slacks, and casual resort style button down shirts. The shorter of the two had thick, long blond hair that just brushed his collar, and a short-trimmed beard. As she watched him from her seat, she noticed the rigid line of displeasure of his jaw when the woman he was with placed a possessive hand on his arm and pulled them to a stop. The haughty bitch informed him, "You didn't tell me you were staying in this part of town. I demand we move to The Four Seasons."

Emma picked up her New York accent, recognizing it was people like this who gave all Americans a bad reputation abroad. She enjoyed the front row seat to the drama playing out in front of her.

"Excuse me? You demand? Last time I checked, you hadn't paid for as much as a cup of café au lait in the last two days. I've about had it with your demands Christy."

Christy's friend decided to do some demanding of her own. "Jaxson, are you going to let Chase talk to Christy like that?" She leaned in to stroke her manicured hand that was dripping with jewels down the chest of the dark haired, taller man.

Emma was beginning to think the ability to pick up on body language and being a spoiled rich-bitch was mutually exclusive because like Bianca before them, these two women were clueless to the fact that the handsome men they were with were about to blow a gasket as they both continued to disparage the more than beautiful lobby of the Marriott they were currently making a scene in the middle of.

The blond muscular hunk named Chase blew first, taking the bitch's hand from his arm. "You know what, I think you had a fabulous idea there, Christy." The woman was silly enough to break into a victorious smile, thinking she'd won the argument when it was clear she was about to be dumped. "You and Liz head on over to the Four Seasons."

She finally faltered. "But, aren't you and Jax coming too?"

"I don't think so. In fact, this is going to be where we part ways."

"But... "

Jaxson had taken a step away from the other bitch with pencil straight hair and equally flat chest. "That goes for you too, Liz. We're done."

"Why, I never... And just who is going to pay for our rooms?"

Chase chuckled. "We were with you two days ago when you each got a ten thousand dollar wire from your daddies. I suggest you use some of that."

"Don't be silly. That's our shopping money."

"Fine by us. Maybe you'll find a shop that will let you sleep on their floor. Not our problem."

Emma wanted to clap for the dramatic show the rich girls were portraying as they pretended to be surprised. The bellman was about to pass them on the way to the elevator with all of their bags, but Jaxson stopped him, retrieving two and leaving the rest on the cart. He pulled out a twenty-euro bill and handed it to the bellman.

"The ladies have unfortunately had something come up and won't be staying after all. Please take this tip to help them back to the front door to hail a cab." He turned to the women and gave them an unemotional farewell. "Safe travels."

The men each grabbed their bag and boarded the next elevator while the now-deserted women stood in shock. Feeling lighter than she had a few minutes before, Emma rose to go to her own room and pack.

CHAPTER 2

*E*mma left for the train station early the next morning to ensure she had enough time to find the correct train to Paris. Since Emma didn't have the two-hundred and fifty euros needed to spend another night at the Marriott in Nice, she needed to head to Paris a day early.

The taxi ride took most of her remaining cash, and she had only one more coach ticket left on her Eurail pass, which also meant she could check her biggest bag, but she had to schlep her own huge backpack onboard to sit in the crowded seats. She tried not to think about where she was going to sleep her final night in Paris.

In the hour before the train left, Emma went in search of a pastry and latte for breakfast. She was careful to steer clear of the pack of rough-looking teenagers who were harassing some young, cute college-age women who were speaking German. She didn't need that added aggravation.

As she waited, several announcements were made in French over the PA system. Emma panicked when some of the people waiting with her got up to leave. Was her train delayed or was it moved to leave from another track? As she glanced around nervously trying to figure it out, she caught a glimpse of the two hot guys, Jaxson and Chase, from the Marriott the night before. They seemed more casual today now that they'd lost the sticks of women who'd been with them earlier.

Something about them felt so familiar. It was more than recognizing them from the hotel. Observing how others watched and pointed at them as they passed, Emma put together that she'd seen them before. She searched her memory trying to place them.

Knowing they were American and spoke English, Emma wished she were brave enough to ask them for help in finding her train, but that wasn't in the cards. She'd dated a few guys back home in Wisconsin, but these men were in a whole other league. Put her up against anyone in academics, and Emma was unstoppable. Put her in a sexual situation, and Emma crumbled. At least she was intelligent enough to know it would be impossible to speak to the two sexiest men she'd ever seen in person without making a complete fool of herself.

She'd been so entranced watching the two good-looking men, she'd completely lost track of the four rowdy teenagers until she found them surrounding her, reaching out to grope her as they spoke French she couldn't understand.

"Knock it off! Leave me alone!" Emma elbowed the largest of the four when he leaned in, rubbing up against her as she felt him fumbling for her purse. At least she'd hidden her passport and plane ticket carefully, but she couldn't afford to lose the last few Euros she had.

When she felt hands feeling up her breasts from behind, she stopped protecting her money, worried the hoodlums had something more sinister than theft in mind. Her fear was confirmed as they worked in unison to start dragging her towards a nearby private locker area. Emma knew if they got her somewhere hidden, anything could happen. She flailed with all of her strength, but the laughing teens only gripped her harder and moved faster, lifting her off the ground and carrying her towards the lockers.

Emma filled her lungs with air and screamed as loud as possible, trying to make enough of a scene that the hoodlums would release her. All that happened was a dirty hand got clamped over her mouth to try to stifle her. She bit her assailant, dragging what she assumed was a French curse word from him.

She closed her eyes and tried to think of how she'd get out of this mess. They'd almost succeeded in getting her alone when she was unceremoniously dropped the few feet to the concrete. She landed on her ass first, but when the guy supporting her head let go too, it crashed back to connect with the unforgiving floor with a crack.

Through her confusion, she found herself curled up in the middle of a fistfight happening all around her. She wondered if she was dreaming as she watched the two American hotties punch out two of the assailants. It took them seconds to send all four of the teens running in different directions.

The most beautiful green eyes she had ever seen peered down at her. She was mesmerized by their intensity long enough that she didn't realize his mouth was moving too.

"I think we need to call a doctor. She appears unresponsive." Green-eyes spoke. What was his name again? John? Jim?

"Okay, I'll go in search of help." She recognized that deep voice.

She eventually snapped out of it to answer them. "I only bumped my head."

I only bumped my head.

Those were the best first words she could come up with when talking to the two hottest men on the planet? The bump on her head wasn't making it any easier to speak intelligently.

"I mean you don't need to get a doctor. I'll be fine."

She wasn't prepared for the dark-haired hottie to scold her.

"What the hell were you doing letting them surround you? Beautiful women traveling alone need to pay more attention."

Had he used the word beautiful as he spoke of her? He must not have gotten a good look at her.

She felt his hand lifting her to gently feel the back of her head, checking for injuries. His fingers massaged her scalp sending tingles throughout her body. "You have the start of a goose-egg there. We'd better get you an ice pack and some Tylenol. Can you sit up?"

Emma didn't trust her voice so she nodded. His blond friend kneeled on the other side of her and together the men gently pulled her to a sitting position. She saw stars for a few seconds, but was surprised to see lingering concern on their handsome faces.

She finally found her voice. "Th...thank you. I don't know what would have happened if you hadn't helped me."

"Yeah, well Roberta will kick our ass if she finds out we threw punches. Let's keep that our secret, okay?" Green-eyes smiled a devastatingly playful grin.

Emma must have hit her head harder than she thought. "Who is Roberta?"

"Our agent and manager."

Still nothing.

Brown-eyes answered as he felt her bump. "We're models here in Europe for a series of shoots. We're on our way to Paris for the last one and we wouldn't hear the end of it if we'd got our asses kicked two days before reporting to set."

So they were models.

"What's your name?" Brown-eyes probed.

"Why?"

"Because we loved how you dealt with that bitch friend of yours yesterday at the Marriott."

"You saw that?" Emma's voice squeaked with surprise.

"Yeah, just like we know you were watching as we gave those bitches we were with the boot."

The dark-haired guy took charge, the playful grin gone. "Still waiting for your name."

It was a demand. "Emma."

"Well, Emma. Let's get you on your feet. They moved our train to another track so we'd better get a move on."

"What do you mean our train?" How did they know where she was going?

"You're going to Paris, right?"

"Yeah," she answered.

"Then let's go."

She felt a surge of bravery. "Wait. You have to tell me your names, too."

"I'm Jaxson and this is Chase. Now let's go."

They pulled her to her feet and even grabbed her heavy backpack for her. She could have walked on her own, but there was no way she was going to tell them since they had each grabbed her arms and were helping her back through the growing crowds.

She didn't miss the jealous glances in her direction from almost every woman they passed. She assumed the men were heading towards the proper platform, but in that moment, she didn't care. She was too busy enjoying their proximity.

A train was pulling into the station when they arrived at the appointed track. The men didn't let go of her the entire ten minutes they waited for arriving passengers to disembark. A charged energy fell over the linked threesome as they waited. She felt it odd they wouldn't try to distance themselves from her, the plump grad student from Wisconsin. All she could think about was how she had to be ruining their GQ reputation.

When passengers were finally allowed to begin loading, she pressed forward into the crowd along with the men, until they moved to pass the closest coach car. Emma dug in her heels to try to stop them. "I have a coach ticket. I need to board there."

"You shouldn't be alone in case you have a concussion. We have a private car with plenty of room. You should ride with us. You'll be more comfortable and we'd like to keep an eye on you." Jaxson's deep voice melted over her, drawing her in.

Emma was in shock. While on one level she was thrilled to spend more time with the two hottest men on the planet, something wasn't sitting right with her. Why would they want to spend time with her when they could snap their fingers and have any woman within fifty yards?

"I don't think that's a good idea. I can't afford an upgrade." She shuffled self-consciously.

They had already moved past the pressing crowd, merging with a smaller, more selective clientele heading to the first class cars. Emma pulled at Jaxson's arm, once again trying to slow their forward progress until the men stopped, pulling her aside to let others pass.

Before she knew what was happening, Emma felt her back pressed against the concrete pillar while the men moved closer. Jaxson leaned in intimately so he could be heard over the commotion of the station. He towered over her, bending to put his face inches from hers. The protective look in his green-eyes took her breath away.

"Now, Emma. We know you don't speak French, are short on cash and are in need of an escort to get you safely to Paris. More importantly, you need to be monitored to make sure you don't have a concussion. We have the space and would be honored if you'd let us take care of you for the next few hours."

"You? Honored? Hours?" Her voice quavered.

Just great. They'd reduced her to single word sophomoric responses. As she weighed her options, she let her eyes wander to the huge advertising posters lining the nearby station wall. Her heart lurched as she recognized the two men currently brushing her arm intimately as the same two models at the center of the upscale men's fashion spread.

13

When Jaxson reached for her hand, twining his fingers through her own intimately to lead her towards the waiting first-class car, Emma had a premonition she might have averted one dangerous situation, only to land herself in even more trouble.

CHAPTER 3

$\mathcal{W}$hen they'd said they had a private car, she'd assumed they meant a small private berth, but they were ushered to a suite, which took up close to a whole car. She hadn't even suspected such luxurious accommodations existed on the train.

A personal butler was waiting, having already prepared the room for their arrival. The decor was a rich, dark mahogany with a deep red carpet. Her heart rate spiked as she took in the queen-sized bed filling one wall. There was also a small dining table, which sat four in front of the wall of windows. A tray of meats and cheeses was already laid out waiting for them. The wall opposite the bed had a large flat screen TV in the center and was surrounded by shelves holding books, games, DVD's and expensive looking knick-knacks. A long couch faced the TV, dividing the space and a small door to the left probably led to a private bathroom.

Once again, Jaxson took the lead. "We'd like a bottle of your best champagne brought in along with a carafe of orange juice and a fruit tray."

"Yes, sir. Right away, sir." The butler left in a hurry to do his bidding.

Emma wasn't exactly sure what to do with herself, but Chase solved the problem by leading her by her elbow to the bed. "You should lay down for a bit to make sure you don't get a headache from the bump you got."

The feminist in her wanted to tell the men she could take care of herself, but in all honesty, it felt wonderful to be taken care of just this once. He helped her lay back on the pillows. She only protested when he reached to slip off her sandals and start rubbing her feet.

"What are you doing?"

"Helping you relax."

"What if I don't want to relax?"

His eyes snapped up to hers, a sexy grin on his face. "Of course you want to relax, Emma. Let me help you."

He stated it as if it were the most natural thing in the world. The funny thing was, him massaging her feet did help her loosen up, something she never thought she'd do in the presence of the two models.

As she lay there watching Jaxson and Chase in the opulent space, Emma had a distinct feeling she'd left reality and had been thrown into an alternate universe. That had to be the only explanation for how she found herself here with these two extraordinary men.

The threesome said little while they waited for the butler to return. Jaxson busied himself rummaging through his suitcase near the closet while Chase helped her to unwind with his magic fingers. Only after the butler had laid out the food and drinks and had been dismissed by Jaxson, did the atmosphere change.

It started with Jaxson following the uniformed man to the door and distinctly locking it behind him. The click of the lock got her pulse thumping. The look on Jaxson's face as he turned to watch her and Chase would have knocked her on her ass had she been standing.

She watched silently as he opened the bottle of champagne. The sharp pop of the cork startled her. The room was so quiet; she could make out the sound of the bubbles as Jaxson poured three flutes to the three-quarters mark before reaching for the OJ and filling them to make mimosas. His eyes bored into her as he approached the bed where she and Chase lounged, the drinks in tow. He held a glass out silently to her, nodding for her to reach out and take it.

Emma noticed Chase did Jaxson's silent bidding, sitting up to take his own drink. Jaxson finally spoke, raising his glass in a toast. "To new friends."

Both men drank, but Emma sat frozen, her back against the pillows stacked along the headboard. "You aren't drinking, Emma. Don't you like meeting new friends?" Jax stared as he waited for her answer. She'd never met someone this intense before.

"Is that what we are? Friends?" Where did that question come from?

Jax finally cracked a small smile, "Of course we're friends. Don't think we invite everyone we meet into our private car."

"I'm not complaining, mind you, but why did you do that, exactly?"

Jax's green eyes twinkled with a mischief she hadn't seen there before. "I don't think she trusts us, Chase. What do you think?"

She tore her gaze from Jax to see Chase grinning at her. Her skin felt on fire where his left hand was now caressing her left ankle, moving slowly higher under her jeans to her calf as he lifted his glass with his other hand to his lips to sip the drink before answering. "I think you're right, Jax. What a shame, too. We are very trustworthy kinda guys." The heated look on his face told her they were anything but.

Despite the alarm bells going off in her head, Emma was filled with a foreign desire to live dangerously. Yesterday she'd concluded she needed to start taking more risks. It wasn't every day she had a chance to make friends with two hot models.

"Trustworthy, you say. I'd have to say so far, that might be true considering you saved me from the goons in the station and have helped me recover from their attack. Still... you haven't mentioned what you expect in return for your kindness."

Jaxson answered with an exaggerated tone, which told her he was playing with her. "I resent that. We want to help out a beautiful woman and get accused of wanting something in return."

Emma's self-doubt ran deep. The words spilled out of her mouth without even thinking, "Ha! Now I know you are liars. I'm not beautiful. At least not like those two models you were with yesterday at the hotel. I'm fat and plain and..."

He moved so swiftly she barely had time to understand what was happening. She felt Chase's hand squeezing her ankle as if to hold her still while Jax put his drink down on the bedside table before leaning in close. His hands brushed her body sending an electric shock through her, as she smelled his minty breath as he chastised her. All traces of his smile were gone, replaced by a scowl.

"That will be the last time you call yourself fat... or plain... Do you hear me?"

Her heart pounded in her chest by the serious anger she saw flashing in his eyes. "Why are you so angry? I'm only saying the truth."

Emma truly didn't understand the rules of the game the men seemed to be playing. They sat in silence for a full minute, the atmosphere growing more awkward by the second. By the time Jaxson spoke, she knew whatever came out of his mouth would be the truth. She saw him struggling to find his words.

"You honestly don't see it, do you?"

"See what?"

"How beautiful you are."

She snickered, yet a small part of her obsessed over how

awesome it would be to have those words be true. "Listen, you guys are nice, but you don't have to keep lying."

She was on her feet in a flash, pulled there by Jaxson before he led her to the full-length mirror on the sliding closet door. Jax was a full foot taller than her. Their gaze met in the mirror as he held her still in front of him with his hands on her hips.

"Do you want to know what I see, Emma?" He didn't wait for her reply.

His right hand stroked her long, thick brunette hair, weaving his fingers through what she considered her best physical attribute. Surprise arced through her when he yanked it, pulling her head back and exposing her creamy neck to the man who suddenly looked like a predator. "This is extraordinary hair, Emma. It makes me want to run my fingers through it and use it as a handle while I fuck you from behind."

His shocking words branded her, but he wasn't done. His left hand moved to cup her double D breast, drawing a groan from her when he pinched her nipple, helping it to protrude obscenely through her thin top. "Did you see the pathetic breasts the bitch I was with yesterday had? They didn't even fill half my hand. I could spend hours tying up and playing with your tits, baby. Skinny girls don't have what you have."

It was a toss up whether her heart or brain was racing faster at Jaxson's unexpected statement. Could he be telling the truth that he not only overlooked her less than perfect body, but actually valued it?

Chase had joined them at the mirror and spoke next. "It's your lips I can't stop thinking about. You have the most beautiful, full lips. I would give anything to have you on your knees in front of me, looking up from below while you wrapped those pretty, perfect lips around my cock."

Jaxson had to see the surprise in her reflection because he jumped in again. "You're a natural beauty, Emma. You don't need tons of makeup and designer clothes to hide behind. But, it was your gorgeous eyes that attracted me to you first. They are the most unique shade of violet. In our business, everyone lies. I've learned how to read people through their eyes to try to pick out the bullshit. Your eyes are a mirror into your soul, Emma."

She braved speaking for the first time, "And what do my eyes say to you?" Her voice quavered. She wasn't sure what she was hoping for.

His mischievous grin was back. "They tell me you want to believe me. I see your intelligence... your honesty... your desire to be the one in the limelight for once instead of the one sitting on the sidelines."

That hit a bit too close to home for Emma. How could this man possibly know how she had been feeling since coming to Europe? Jax's gaze flashed with satisfaction. "I have your attention now, don't I little girl?"

It was as if he had a playbook to her heart. Emma was consumed with a desire she hadn't felt before. It went deeper than sexual need. Stronger than physical desires. More powerful than mere mental images. The urge felt as if it came from her very core – a base, human level she was incapable of resisting. The only word she could think of in the moment was submission.

It was absurd. She barely knew these men. She didn't know where they were from or how old they were. She didn't even know their last names. They could be serial killers or rapists for all she knew, but in that moment, she had fallen under their spell. She'd blame it on them drugging her, but she hadn't taken her first sip of mimosa yet.

She felt the train lurching forward, leaving the safety of the station. The parallel to the moment happening in the luxury cabin was ironic. As they picked up speed, so did her heart rate. With each block they traveled away from the station, Emma felt herself moving away from her comfort zone.

Jaxson broke the silence. "Six hours. We'll be pulling into Paris in six short hours." His hands were back on her hips, his chin above her right shoulder so he could lean in to whisper seductively into her ear. "I want you to turn yourself over to Chase and me until we pull into Paris. I promise you, Emma; you won't regret it."

She already knew she would be saying yes to whatever it was they were offering; yet she felt the need to at least ask. "What does that mean? Turn myself over to you?"

It was Chase who spoke, moving in front of her to sandwich her between the two men. He pressed close enough until she felt the warmth of both men as Chase cupped her face, holding her firmly to ensure he had her full attention. "Exactly as it sounds. Jaxson and I have particular *activities* we enjoy participating in together. We've learned we both enjoy these activities best when shared with others. Unfortunately, we trust few people to join in our fun."

"You trust me?"

"We do."

"What if I decide I don't approve of your... *activities?*"

Jax wasn't playing fair. His lips had attached to the tender spot where her neck met her shoulder. He nipped her playfully while trailing nibbling kisses down her shoulder before lifting his head and speaking softly into her ear.

"I guarantee you'll love every single thing we do to you, Emma, but regardless, all you need to do is safeword and we'll stop."

She'd read her share of racy romance novels. She might live the life of a straight-laced prude, but she masturbated to the fodder her favorite erotic romances offered. Not even in her wildest dreams did she think she'd ever be in a situation where a safeword would be required.

"Do you know what a safeword..."

She cut him off. "Puppy."

"Excuse me?"

"I always thought puppy would make an appropriate safeword." She tried to hide her smile.

Both men chuckled, and Chase responded. "I see you've given this some thought. That's a good sign. Puppy it is."

The tension in the air shifted with the last short sentence, as if the negotiations were over. Consent had been provided. Emma's heart pounded with anticipation. She didn't have to wait long.

Jax's voice gave Chase direction. "Let's get her naked."

Six hours, Emma. Let go and enjoy these six short hours.

CHAPTER 4

*T*he next few minutes passed in slow motion. Emma tried to stay in the moment, but it was difficult when her mind kept screaming the logical reasons why what she was doing was risky – why she should run from the room, never to look back. She had no intention of listening to those voices. She didn't feel in danger. She felt alive.

She stood limp and loose, letting four large hands roam across her skin unchecked. Caresses, pinches, kisses and a few small slaps trailed across her body as each stitch of clothing was slowly peeled from her. She closed her eyes, allowing herself to absorb each touch. It felt as if her pilot light had been lit and the men were slowly stoking her fire hotter with each nip and groan. She lost herself to the physical rapture of being the center of their talented attention.

She stood naked before them, putting off opening her eyes because she knew it would make her feel self-conscious. Jax hugged her from behind, allowing his large hands to roam, pinching her breasts until her tits protruded and giving Chase the perfect place to latch onto. He wasn't gentle as he pulled her left nipple into his warm mouth, sucking hard as if he might extract mother's milk that wasn't there. His hands massaged her heavy breasts while Jax moved lower.

She pushed down the embarrassment she felt when Jax squeezed the love handles on her hips, moving one hand to palm her rounded tummy before trailing lower. He let loose a sexy growl in her right ear as he stroked his fingers through her neatly trimmed hair to sink into her slick and wet pussy.

"Fuck, you're so wet. I can't wait to taste you, Emma."

She could smell the proof of her physical excitement in the air. It made her feel strangely powerful. The men may be in control of the scene, but it was her body causing the erection she felt poking her from behind. There was no doubt Jaxson was enjoying himself. She shivered with need, wanting that massive cock inside her and suspecting she'd need to wait.

Jaxson's next order surprised her. "Chase... your turn. Strip for us." She wasn't sure if it was his inflection or the use of the word *us*, but Emma sensed Jaxson intended to enjoy the sight of his friend naked as much as he enjoyed undressing Emma. She opened her eyes as Chase stepped back a few feet, locking Jaxson with a heated stare as he started to unbutton his dress shirt slowly. With each button, his gaze turned more feral and for the first time since they left the station, Emma felt left out, as the two men were lost in each other.

Chase had the chest of a body builder, muscular and defined with a smattering of light chest hair. He could double for a California surfer with his tanned, toned body, and shoulder length blond hair. He hadn't taken the time to shave. She could make out the small dimple on his chin. His brown eyes snapped from Jaxson back to Emma as his hands moved to his wide belt buckle. Just like that, she was pulled back into the scene.

The distinctive sound of him pulling the leather through the loops ending in a sharp snap as the top of the belt swung free caused her heart to skip a beat. Emma spent more time than she should watching spanking videos on the Internet. She'd dreamed of being disciplined by a leather belt more times than she could count and apparently her face portrayed her desire because Chase grinned down at her.

"We hit the jackpot, Jax. She's a spanko."

She wanted to protest, but it would be a lie and as weird as this whole situation was, she didn't want to lie to the men. Jaxson's lips on her ear brought a full-out tremor to her body. "That news makes me a happy man, Emma."

Her words tumbled out, unchecked. "Yes, sir."

Chase's snug jeans hit the floor next, leaving only his boxer briefs. Emma licked her lips subconsciously when she realized his cock was so large it extended beyond the elastic waistband, a drop of pre-cum glistened in the light shining through the large window.

The train was moving quickly enough now the scenery outside flashed by. She knew no one would be able to see inside the car, but regardless, with the curtains pulled back, it felt as if the three of them were on a fast moving stage, on display for anyone who might care to look close enough.

When Chase stood naked, he sought out Jaxson as if looking for direction. Seems they were both under the dark-haired dominant's command. Her pussy contracted with need as she took in the oversized erection protruding from Chase's body. It was by far the thickest cock she'd ever seen in her inexperienced life.

Jax's order brought her back to the present. "On your knees, Emma. Chase wants to see those beautiful lips of yours wrapped around the base of his cock."

She fell to her knees without question, anxious to please these mighty men. When she reached out to touch Chase, Jaxson corrected her. "No hands. Wrap your arms behind your back, grab your elbows and don't let go. Chase will be in control."

While she didn't have an extraordinary amount of practice with this particular activity, her excitement in the moment had saliva filling her mouth in anticipation. She felt her long hair being fashioned into a ponytail by Jax and handed to Chase as he reached out. He pulled her forward roughly as he took a step closer, closing the distance between them.

Emma first used her tongue to lick the glob of pre-cum from the tip of his cock. She might be on her knees, but she had never felt more powerful than she did when realizing Chase's legs were trembling precariously. Her tongue swished circles across the tip of his cock until he couldn't wait any longer and yanked her forward as he slipped between her lips, pressing in deeper than she was prepared for on a first thrust. Emma gurgled as his rigid member rubbed the back of her throat. Their intimacy grew as he began to slide in and out, fucking her mouth. His grip on her hair tightened as his excitement drove him faster.

"Eyes." It was Chase directing her to look up from her perch below. The fire in his own eyes was intoxicating and only flamed hotter when Jax did his own ordering. "Eyes."

Suddenly they were all connected in an intimate way, which only grew as Jaxson leaned forward in slow motion. Emma almost choked when the two men's lips connected in a hot, open-mouth kiss above her. She'd been prepared for them both to dominate her body, but she was surprised when Jaxson turned the men's kiss almost violent, dominating Chase.

It was Jax who stopped the action by pulling out of their kiss. "Step back, Chase. You and Emma need to wait longer before you're allowed come."

Chase didn't seem bothered in the least. His now wet cock slapped against the perfect V of his groin.

She could hear Jax undressing behind her, but since he hadn't instructed her to move, she remained still, anticipating what their next surprise might be.

She felt the warmth of Jax leaving to go towards the bed. Chase helped her to her feet and they followed. Jax had laid down in the center of the large bed, and like Chase, he was tan all over. If possible, his cock was even longer than his friend's.

He was still in control. "Chase, you know what to do. Emma, come sit on my face facing Chase. I wouldn't want you to miss any of the excitement."

She moved to follow his direction, watching Chase out of the corner of her eye. Once she had straddled above Jax, she realized she had a front row seat to the show. Just as she had done before him, Chase locked his arms behind his back and was leaning over Jax's demanding cock. Jax guided the tip of his cock into Chase's open mouth where it disappeared completely as Chase deep throated the entire erection in one thrust.

"Emma." Jax's stern use of her name brought her back to the moment. She lowered her wet pussy to his waiting lips, shuddering as his tongue grazed her clit. Jax ate her with the same gusto Chase was using to pleasure Jaxson's cock.

The three of them were intimately linked in a way Emma couldn't have imagined. The sight of Jax's cock disappearing deep into Chase's waiting mouth was the hottest damn thing she'd ever seen. The gagging sounds as the protrusion hit the back of his throat added to the ambience of the moving cabin.

She was having so much fun watching, she almost forgot to enjoy what was happening to her own body. Jax must have suspected because his hands reached up to hold her against him while he slid his tongue in and out of her crease. She reached down to rub her own clit, her fingers sliding easily through the copious lubrication. The look of lust on Chase's face as he watched her, his throat full of cock, sent her into a shuddering orgasm.

Chase leaned up grinning, spittle on his chin. "Uh-oh. You're a naughty girl. No one comes until Jaxson approves it."

She was coming around, finally able to talk. "That's not fair. You didn't tell me that rule."

Jaxson sat up, grinning. "I'll let the first one pass, but no more now that you know."

"But... what if..."

"Ask for permission. Maybe I'll say yes." This playful version of the dominant man was intoxicating. His eyes twinkled with a mischief as he reached out to pull her into an open mouth kiss. She tasted herself as his tongue tangled with her own. When he pulled out of their kiss, he demanded the words she had been hoping for. "I need to be inside you, Emma. On your hands and knees."

Emma moved quickly to follow directions. She'd expected Jaxson to take his spot behind her, but was surprised when Chase moved into position on his knees in front of her, placing his still stiff cock back against her lips. She couldn't see either man's face, but she suspected they were silently communicating because they both filled her in one swift thrust. Her scream of surprise at Jaxson's large cock bottoming out inside her was drowned out by the manhood hitting the back of her throat, gagging her.

She felt overwhelmed as both pleasure and pain combined in an unexpected way. She pushed down the urge to laugh as she thought of the pitiful lovers she'd had back in Wisconsin with their inexperienced fumbling in the dark, unable to pleasure her the way she'd wanted. Now she had not one, but two experienced men working her body over in a way, which promised to deliver pleasure, at least for the remaining time they had together. A pang of something she didn't want to examine constricted her heart and she pushed it aside to concentrate on the pounding she was receiving.

Jaxson's erection was perfection – long, hard and thick. He leaned forward, changing the angle of his insertion and almost tipped her into another orgasm.

She pulled her face away from Chase long enough to shout out, "May I come?"

"No, you may not," was his brisk answer. Chase filled her mouth again quickly.

She pouted, until she realized the angle of his insertion was different too. Over the loud slapping sounds in the small room, she could make out the sounds of their open mouth kissing and sucking above her. All three bodies were linked together in a triangle of sex.

She tasted his pre-cum and knew Chase was close to coming. Jaxson's voice sounded almost manic when he asked her quickly, "Are you on the pill?"

Chase pulled out long enough for her to grunt out a short, "Yes!" He was back inside her one second later.

"Together. We're all going to come together. Now!"

He didn't have to tell her twice. Emma shattered with ecstasy, enhanced by the feeling of Jaxson's fingers digging into her hips as he held her tightly, depositing his cum deep inside her hot pussy as Chase spurted his salty mix down her throat. She choked on the volume.

The three of them collapsed to the bed in a sweaty mess, recovering in their own way, yet each reaching out to caress the flesh closest to them.

A couple of intense minutes passed. She waited to start feeling like a third wheel in what was clearly already a solid relationship, but the awkwardness didn't come. Jaxson rolled to his side to face them, placing his head in his left hand to prop himself up above them. A wave of satisfaction washed through Emma as she realized she was at least partly responsible for that sexy smile on his face.

"Damn, it's been a long time since it felt that fantastic. My intuition was right about you, Emma. You're special."

She still didn't believe him, but she'd at least learned not to disagree out loud. She didn't want to sound stupid, but she had to ask.

"So you guys... are... a couple?"

She didn't miss the heated look the men shared. "It's not that simple. We were friends first, each having had a few relationships over the years. We decided to experiment a bit, feeling a mutual attraction. It's complicated. We rarely play with just the two of us.

It's weird, but we found it's best between us when we share each other with a woman."

Emma giggled. "Somehow I can't picture those sticks you were with back in Nice wanting to share either of you."

"Oh Christ, no way. We met them in Paris last week and decided to take them with us on our weekend off. Colossal mistake. We should have stayed in Paris." Jaxson sounded disgusted with how his weekend had gone.

Chase disagreed. "I'm not sorry." They both glanced at him questioningly when he broke out with a grin. "We wouldn't have met Emma if we hadn't gone to Nice."

CHAPTER 5

A couple of hours and several orgasms later, Emma lay cuddled between the two sleeping sex gods who had stumbled into her life unexpectedly. Jaxson's naked body spooned her from behind, his arm wrapped around her waist to hold her close. Chase faced them, his arm draped across them both, linking the three of them even in sleep.

A few hours ago, Emma's biggest concern had been the risk she was taking in having sex with two strangers. How quickly her concern had shifted to how she was going to be able to walk away from them at the train station, never to see them again.

She'd become a woman on this train. There would be no going back to the naive, inexperienced girl she'd been in Nice. She'd collected hundreds of mementos – photos and trinkets – reminders of her trip. But the most important part of her time in Europe – these two men and their precious time together – no souvenir would capture. She'd only have memories of the six hours that changed her life.

It was more than the mind-blowing sex. She felt a calmness that wasn't there before. A confidence. She was no longer the girl who had to stay back at the table to watch the purses while the sexy women danced. No. From now on, she would be on the dance floor. It was someone else's turn to watch the fucking purses.

"Hey. What are you thinking about?" She'd missed Chase waking.

"Nothing."

"Oh no you don't. We haven't lied to each other yet. I'm not letting you start now."

Their eyes connected. She was surprised to see his held the same sadness closing in on her. She never did answer him. There was no need. He already saw the truth.

"Where are you staying when we pull into Paris?"

The panic of having nowhere to stay invaded. "I... I'm not sure yet."

"When is your flight home again?"

"Tomorrow."

"You should stay with us until you fly out."

Emma's first instinct was to jump for joy. It would be so easy to let the men take care of her. They could spend twenty-four hours instead of six having sex.

And then what? It would be even harder to say good-bye. No thanks.

"I don't think that's a good idea."

Chase didn't let it drop. "I think it's a perfect idea. We could..."

"Chase, Emma said no." Jaxson's deep voice startled her. Tears sprang to her eyes; sure he meant he didn't want her to stay with them. "I'm hoping we can change her mind before we pull into the station, of course."

The feeling of relief at his words only made her feel worse. What was happening to her? She barely knew these men, yet she truly hadn't felt happier and safer than she felt at that minute. How would she ever have a chance at finding something this extraordinary again in her life?

The sharp knock on the door startled her, but she sensed the men had been expecting it. As usual, Jax took control. "Time to get cleaned up. Unfortunately, the bathroom here isn't large enough for all of us." He paused. She couldn't see his expression in their spooned position. "Our suite at the hotel, on the other hand, would accommodate all kinds of mutual fun should you decide to change your mind, sweetheart."

He had leaned up to nibble on her neck from above. She giggled when he hit a ticklish spot.

Chase grinned, "See, you're having fun. We don't have to be on our next shoot until the day after tomorrow. Come back to our hotel with us."

Emma closed her eyes, trying to reason her way through the decision. She was more tempted than any other time in her entire twenty-two years. Conservative, sensible, hardworking Emma was at war with this new, adventurous version of herself.

For many, she suspected this would be an easy decision, but she didn't want to risk ruining the absolutely perfect memories she would have of the amazing six hours she once spent on a train between Nice and Paris. Years from now, she knew she would look back at this time as one of the most exciting of her life. If she chose to stay with these two extraordinary men for an additional twenty-four hours, she would risk tarnishing the perfection. What if they tired of her and she began to feel like the third wheel in their world?

But what if she didn't?

To their credit, the men gave her the time she needed to sort through her feelings. When she opened her peepers again, Chase was grinning at her. He already knew her decision.

Jaxson finally pressed her, slipping his hand to squeeze her ample breast as if to emphasize his control over her. "Give us the next twenty-four hours, Emma." It wasn't really a question. It was a statement.

Emma took a deep breath and whispered, "Yes."

She could hear the authority as Jax pressed her. "That didn't seem too confident, baby."

Chase's gaze smoldered with anticipation as she answered submissively, "Yes, sir."

CHAPTER 6

*J*f she thought they'd pampered her on the train, Emma was completely bowled over by their attention as they carried her backpack, helped locate and pull her checked luggage, and escort her to a private livery car that was waiting to whisk them back to a luxury hotel a stone's throw away from the *Champs-Élysées*.

The men sandwiched her between them in the back seat on the drive, taking turns mauling her as if they hadn't just had wild sex multiple times in the last few hours. Not one to sit idle, she put both her hands to work stroking their semi-hard cocks through their slacks until each man was groaning with renewed need.

She should have been mortified when she met the driver's curious eyes in the rearview mirror, but in that moment, Emma felt pure power. As the driver shifted uncomfortably in his seat while they waited for a traffic light, she realized she was responsible for not two, but three, turned on men in the small space.

As the driver's curious look took on a hungry longing, Emma felt Jax leaning in to whisper in her ear. "I told you that you were beautiful, Emma. He wants to fuck you as badly as Chase and I do.

Do you see how jealous he is of me because I get to touch you like this?"

Until then, their petting had been discreet, but Jax moved his hand up under her shirt, lifting it to expose her bra. He lowered his mouth to kiss the swell of her heavy breasts above the lacy fabric as Chase's hand snuck between her legs to expertly find her clit on his first try, despite the yoga pants covering it from view.

Chase whispered in her other ear, "Let's show him how beautiful you are when you come, shall we?"

She wanted to protest and push them way for propriety's sake, but considering she was smashed between two of the sexiest men in the city of lights, there was no chance she was going to put a stop to their impromptu sex show.

Emma closed her eyes, giving herself permission to simply feel. She felt the fabric of her bra being pressed above her boobs, exposing her nipples to the men in the confined space. She felt two wet mouths sucking on each of her tits as Chase's fingers moved into higher gear, working their magic on her sensitive button until she was close to exploding. She still had her arms spread, brushing the tenting pants of the men.

She felt Jaxson's lips leave her pebbled tip long enough to bark a sharp order. "Open your eyes, sweetheart. I want you to look into the eyes of the driver so he can watch you come."

It didn't even dawn on her that she could say no. Since the trio had met, Jax had been in control. The heat that met her gaze as she locked eyes with the voyeur to their sexy scene pushed her into a powerful orgasm. Her pulse pounded in her ears as she allowed pleasure to wash over her.

She floated until they were pulling up into the circular drive of the hotel. Before they exited the car, the driver finally spoke. "There wouldn't be a chance you were looking for another participant in your little party, is there?"

Emma's heart pounded. As flattered as she was, she wanted no part in adding anyone else to their planned tryst. Relief flowed through her at Jaxson's response. "Sorry, but she's all ours. Thanks for the ride, though."

He reached out to hand a large tip to the driver before piling out of the door the doorman held open for them.

The walk through the lobby was surreal. She'd stayed in a couple of upscale hotels while traveling with Bianca, but the opulence surrounding them as they moved through the lobby was intimidating. The bellman carried all of their bags, leaving the men's hands free to capture each of hers and hold on tight. The linked threesome drew attention from the curious guests.

As they approached the elevator, two stunningly beautiful women who had to be models exited. They were nearly as tall as the men and thin as boards. They were dressed casually in low riding yoga pants and revealing camisoles with their tiny tits barely peeking through the translucent fabric. It was their boney hip and collarbones that reminded Emma how different she was from the women the men hung out with while modeling.

She didn't miss their surprise at seeing the men holding hands with Emma. She watched their brows narrow as they drew closer. The tallest brunette spoke first.

"It's about time you guys got back. We've been holding off starting the party until you got here. I'm glad you ditched those skanks you left with, but I see you...well look busy."

Emma was relieved the guys seemed anxious to get away from the models.

"We're busy. We'll see you on the set." Jaxson moved them closer to the elevator as the women gave Emma a look that could kill a lesser person.

"I can't believe they'd rather spend time with a mercy case like that than us. She must give good head." Their look hadn't hurt, but their hateful words whispered none-too-softly as they skulked away brought tears to Emma's eyes.

The men moved quickly. Jax released Emma's hand as Chase moved to embrace her in his arms as if to protect her from the hurtful words. Jax stepped up to go eye to eye with the stick, surprised anger radiating off him.

"Watch yourself, Mona. I don't take kindly to you dissing things important to me."

Emma saw the jealously flashing on both of the women's faces. "You can't be serious. She's fat!"

Jaxson's laughter was menacing. "You've lost all touch with reality. She's real. She's beautiful and sensual and intelligent. I'm so fucking sick of hanging out with fake bitches who treat everyone else as if they're gum on the bottom of their designer shoes."

"Fake? You didn't seem to think I was too fake when you were fucking me."

As if they hadn't already drawn enough attention to themselves, her shouting obscenities had every single person staring at the altercation. Emma fought back tears, trying to not let it show how wounded she was by their hurtful words and the implications Jax had slept with the stick.

Then it hit her. Of course he had. He could sleep with anyone and everyone he wanted to, including men apparently. He exuded dominance and this yummy sexiness that went farther than his breathtakingly handsome looks.

They froze in a stand off for a few long seconds before Jax moved closer to Mona, while making sure not to touch her. He spoke quietly, but with passion.

"Both of you together aren't equal to one of her. Yeah... I fucked you, but that's all it was. A fast, physical release with a ready hole. Now, if you'll excuse Chase and me, we have a beautiful woman to go make love to."

Jax reached out with his hand and Chase shuffled them forward. Emma self-consciously reached to take the outstretched hand and Jax moved around the model standing stock still, her mouth gaping open in shock, to pull the three of them into the open small elevator. They pressed seven for their floor and let the doors close behind them before the men pinned Emma against the back wall.

Jax apologized. "I'm so sorry, sweetheart. Are you okay?"

Emma didn't trust her voice so she nodded.

Chase jumped in next. "They're just jealous. They've been chasing us for the two weeks we've been in town working together."

Emma found her voice. "Well, I don't want to mess up your plans if you want to..."

Jaxson's mouth closed in for an open mouth kiss to shut her up. By the time the doors of the elevator opened on their floor, he had convinced her he wasn't interested in changing their planned tryst.

"Let's go."

Their room was at the end of the long hallway. She had expected a bedroom, so she was surprised to walk into a living room space with a floor-to-ceiling bowed window with a direct view of the *Arc de Triomphe de l'Étoile* only a few blocks away. There was a seating area with comfortable-looking furniture facing a media center. On the opposite wall there was a small bar area with a mini-fridge. The round wooden table looked like it would seat six for a meal. A desk area was tucked into the corner.

"It's beautiful, but where do you sleep?"

Chase chuckled. "Technically, we each have our own rooms on either side of this parlor, but I have a feeling we'll all be in Jax's king bed for the next twenty-four hours."

Chase released her hand to open the door to the bellman delivering their bags. Once they were alone again, they stood quietly for a moment as if they were waiting for what came next.

Jaxson took charge. "I'll order up some food and drinks. You two go ahead and get started trying out the awesome shower in my room. I'll be in to join you in a few minutes."

Chase led her through the small bedroom with the large bed she knew they would be spending time in later and into a small, but luxurious bathroom. Jax had told them to shower, but when she saw the raised whirlpool tub, she stopped in her tracks. Her expression must have betrayed how much she wanted to sink her tired and sore body into the tub.

Chase chuckled, detouring them towards the whirlpool. He reached down to pull the stopper and started the water filling the tub, which was large enough to accommodate all three of them. He grabbed a bath bomb from the decorative wicker basket, throwing it in. Within seconds, the comforting smell of lavender filled the air.

He turned towards her, a look of mischief on his tan face. "Jax won't mind that we've detoured to the whirlpool, but he won't be amused if he gets here and we're both still dressed. I've been looking forward to peeling these clothes back off you, young lady."

It was her turn to chuckle. "So, do you always do exactly what Jax tells you to do?"

Chase had a twinkle in his eyes as he reached to pull her top over her head. "Not always." He dipped in for a quick kiss before answering. "Sometimes I defy him on purpose so he'll have good reason to punish me. Like you, I enjoy having my ass lit up by his belt."

Her heart rate was racing. "I never said I'd like that," she protested.

"Maybe not with your words, but your eyes gave you away when you watched me take my own belt off. If we're lucky, we can both feel his leather on our ass before the night is over."

Jaxson's voice from the doorway startled them both. "If you two keep dawdling, you can be sure to feel my belt sooner rather than later."

His words had been strict, but he couldn't hide the smirk of his sexy lips as he approached them. Jax reached out to unhook her bra, yet she felt invisible tingles across her ass at the possibility of her first spanking. "Let me help." Once the bra fell to the floor his strong hands cupped her generous globes as he hugged her from behind while Chase went to work pulling her pants down, taking her skimpy panties along with him. She was stripped naked in seconds.

The muscular men undressed quickly while she tried to ignore the bouncing images of her rounded body in the too-many mirrors in the small room. Everywhere she peeked she saw her naked body, feeling self-conscious as she remembered how thin the models they had met in the lobby were. She had to force her mind to focus on the fact the men had chosen her over them.

A naked Chase led her to the tub, helping her step into the center while the well-hung men each stepped in on either side of her. She waited to see how this was going to work. Jax sunk in first to put his back to the far end of the tub, turning her to face away from him and lower herself into his arms. Chase did the same until the three of them were in a row with Jax hugging her, and Emma hugging Chase while he turned the taps off and the jets on. Instantly water swirled around them, intensifying the lavender aroma.

Emma relaxed against Jaxson's hard chest, enjoying how his arms wrapped around her to touch Chase, linking them intimately. They sat silently enjoying the relaxing swirl around them for a few long minutes.

Jaxson's innocent question surprised her. Up until now, they hadn't discussed personal information. "So why don't you tell us where you live, Emma. Where are you going home to tomorrow?"

"I'm from a small town in Wisconsin, but I go to the University of Wisconsin in Madison. I finished my undergrad in business last fall and am going for my masters in economics."

Chase whistled the sort of whistle that told her he was impressed. "We knew you were smart, but damn, you're going for your master's."

"Yeah, well, I haven't earned it yet, although I did get a teacher's assistant position to the head of the department. The only downside is he's making me teach all of his undergrad classes this summer. It's why I need to get home. Classes start next week." She paused before turning the tables on them. "Your turn. Where are you two from and how did you meet?"

The silence stretched long enough she wondered if they were ever going to answer. Chase spoke quietly. "I grew up in California, but when my parents divorced when I was in high school, I moved with my mom back to live with my grandparents in New York. Jaxson and I met our freshman year at NYU."

When Jaxson didn't expound, she pushed. "How about you, Jax? How'd you end up at NYU?"

She wished she could see his face. He was so quiet and she couldn't tell what he was thinking or if he was upset. He eventually spoke, quietly. "I grew up in DC. My dad is a big wig in politics and my mother a socialite there. When I refused to study something that would help me follow in good 'ole dad's footsteps, they got pretty pissed. At least I ended up looking okay so they could parade me out in front of the cameras to look like the All-American family. What a fucking joke."

Chase finished the story. "Jax was a business major, like you, but I was studying photography. It's how I got introduced to a couple of professional photographers and eventually ended up on the other side of the camera. As soon as my agent saw Jax, she went after him hot and heavy to sign on with her. She promised she could keep us both busy year round and so far, she's kept that promise. We've done shoots all over the world. We get to travel and meet new people. We're making good money and staying in luxurious hotels."

"And meeting beautiful models, like Mona, who want you." Emma wasn't sure why she said that and she hated the jealous twinge to her tone.

It was Jax who took over their story. She was relieved her comment seemed to go unnoticed. "I'll be honest, at first it was fun. The parties. The drinking. The drugs. The sex."

With each short sentence, Emma's heart rate increased. What the hell had she gotten into here?

Jaxson's voice sounded melancholy. "It was about a year ago I woke up hung-over in bed with a twig of a woman and I had no clue who she was. The hotel room was trashed. That's the day I started to pay attention to those around me and I didn't like what I saw. Everyone was so fucking fake. They all thought they were so much better than everyone else and that they didn't have to play by any rules. They treated people like shit. It took me a while to realize why I was beginning to hate them all, but then I put it together. They were exactly the same as the fake people I'd grown up around in politics. The hangers-on who used my dad to make money or get their fifteen minutes of fame. Everyone lying to each other, pretending everything in their life was perfect. I'd have quit already if it weren't for Chase. He's the only thing keeping me in the business now. We're saving up cash so we can retire soon. We have big plans for future investments."

She hated the somber, jaded twinge to his voice. She much preferred the dominant, confident Jaxson. Emma regretted asking them to tell her about themselves until Jax buried his face in her long hair, taking a long drag of her scent before calmly speaking. "I don't normally open up about myself Emma. I'm not exactly sure what it is about you, but I feel safe with you."

It was in that moment she finally understood why the men had chosen her to spend this time with them. It was a compliment in the highest measure. She was the antithesis of the skinny, fake models they were forced to work with every day. She wasn't a groupie or hanger-on who was looking to get rich or gain a place in the limelight. She finally believed that what she had thought was her weakness was, after all, what drew the men to her in the first place.

She was *real*.

Feeling lighter than she had a few minutes before, she sighed, enjoying the feel of being sandwiched between the two men, enjoying the relaxing jets of water soothing their well-sexed bodies. The feel of Jaxson's cock swelling against the base of her back told her where his mind had turned in the silence. Testing her theory, she moved her hands down from Chase's chest and encountered his matching erection.

And just like that, it was time for their next round of amazing sex.

Chase grabbed a bath sponge and soaped it up. He took a few minutes to wash himself before standing and turning in the tub to face Emma. Once he was kneeling in front of her, he began to slowly massage the soft soapy sponge across her body. He didn't rush, taking time to touch each intimate part of her body. Not to be outdone, Jax soaped his hands and massaged her heavy breasts until they were squeaky clean. As four masculine hands roamed every inch of her body, Emma felt pampered. Chase's fingers finally found their way to her pussy, paying homage to her womanly folds as he prepared her for their next round of hot fornication.

They'd been so gentle; it startled her when Jaxson yanked her head back by her long hair. A cup of warm, soapy water seeped through her thick locks before he squirted shampoo into his palm and began massaging the soap through her hair. The men worked silently, caring for her as if she were a precious possession. A twinge of panic over how easy it would be to get used to this treatment invaded, but she pushed it down, unwilling to ruin the short time they had together with worry about tomorrow. She would have the rest of her life to analyze what had happened. As long as she was here – alive and part of this amazing trio – she'd focus on the here and now.

When they were all clean, Chase pulled the stopper. The men got out first, drying themselves before helping her from the tub and once again, drying her from head to toe, stopping often to kiss here and nibble there. It was a slow burn of foreplay as they all made the leisurely climb up the ladder of sexual need.

"On your knees, sweetheart. It's my turn to watch those lips around my cock." She didn't hesitate, falling to her knees on the soft white rug. Emma remembered her earlier lesson and linked her arms behind her back, letting Jaxson reach out and pull her forward. "Open nice and wide, Emma. I'm gonna fill you up now."

He was true to his word. Jaxson's cock was already stiff and when the tip edged the back of her throat, there were still several inches she was not able to accommodate. She tried to press deeper, but her gag reflex kicked in. Minutes passed as he fucked her throat, chasing his pleasure. Globs of phlegm spilled out of the corner of her mouth, spilling down to her breasts. His fingers weaved through her damp, long hair, using his grip to help control the pace.

He pushed her hard until she was short of breath, allowing her brief breaks to gasp for air. The longer she had to focus on servicing Jaxson there on her knees, the deeper she surrendered to her own submission.

Their gaze had been locked throughout the intimate act linking their bodies. Only when she felt Chase's naked erection pressing against the back of her head did Jaxson break their visual connection. Like earlier on the train, the men began to kiss above her. She watched as they began with a slow, gentle loving kiss. She could see their tongues dueling with each other. Jaxson's thrusts in her mouth became more sporadic the more violent the kiss became above her. She watched Chase reach out to pinch each of Jaxson's nipples, dragging a groan from the dominant in the room.

The sound of dishes clinking in the living room of the suite panicked Emma. She was suddenly self-conscious, afraid a hotel housekeeper would walk in on them and as frightening as that sounded, the possibility of being caught increased all of their enjoyment in the moment. Just as when the livery driver was witnessing her orgasm, the idea of having an audience had her own juices flowing.

It was eventually Jaxson who put a stop to the fun. "I think dinner is here. Let's go eat, shall we?" He grinned at her when she let an exasperated groan fill the room.

Emma had a hard time putting the brakes on their sexy scene so abruptly. Their excitement was denied in lieu of foraging for food. The men wrapped her in a fluffy white robe, even taking the time to comb out her hair before finding robes of their own.

The food Jaxson had ordered was a perfect blend of light and heavy, sweet and savory. Their conversation turned to much lighter topics as they enjoyed the food and company. By the time they finished eating, they were all drowsy. Jaxson led them to the bed and after shucking their robes, they fell into a pile of inter-twined flesh, falling into an easy sleep.

CHAPTER 7

*E*mma awoke before midnight to the heavenly feeling of two mouths exploring her body. She didn't open her eyes, choosing to bask in one mouth kissing its way from a protruding nipple through the valley between her ample globes to the other pebbled tit. The second warm mouth placed kisses along her inner thighs as he pushed her legs farther and farther apart to give him access to her sexual core. Her body hummed with need.

She bucked her bottom off the bed when two thick digits thrust into her wet cunt, curling to immediately hit her G-spot. It was as if he had a playbook to her body, bringing her to an almost instant orgasm as she cried out. The mouth kissing her nipple bit down lightly, extending her climax. It was Jaxson's tsking his disappointment she'd come without permission that finally brought her eyes open.

The sight of Chase's lust filled expression from between her legs had her ready to come again. He didn't look sorry in the least that he'd wrung an unapproved release from her.

Jaxson's stern reprimand snapped her out of her sexual haze in a hurry. "That was very naughty. Chase, I hold you responsible for instigating Emma's clear disobedience in coming without permission. We've been together long enough, you should know the rules. You've both earned some attention from my leather belt to hopefully teach you a lesson."

Emma almost came again from the mere implication of his words. She had dreamed of being across a man's lap many times, yet now that the possibility it might happen in reality closed in, she wasn't so sure she could go through with it.

When Jaxson pulled her from the bed their gaze met, and she saw a heated power emanating from him as he slipped deeper into his dominant persona. For the first time since they'd met, the word *puppy* was on the tip of her tongue. She was confidant Jax would stop if she used her safeword. Knowing today might be her only chance to ever give spanking a try, she held her tongue.

Jaxson reached to pull Chase from the bed and for the briefest of seconds, the three of them stood in a group embrace. It was quickly disbanded when Jaxson spun the mischievous duo, pressing the upper half of their backs forward towards the bed until their faces mashed into the messed sheets.

He continued to set the scene. "Spread your legs wide. I want to see your lady bits and hard package clearly. If I'm lucky, I'll land a few stripes in a few delicate areas to help make my point." Once he had them far enough apart and situated the way he wanted, he made one final demand. "I want your eyes open and on each other the whole time. You'll watch each other closely as you're both disciplined, is that understood?"

Emma thought it was a rhetorical question, yet Chase snapped a quick "Yes, sir." Only when she felt Jaxson's open palm crack against her butt did she realize he had expected a reply. She added on her own quick, "Yes, sir."

"Better. We'll get you trained yet."

When Jaxson stepped away from them, Chase slid his right hand closer to place it over her own trembling left hand. He whispered to her, "It will be okay. He won't really hurt us, you know."

She wished she were so sure. She was relieved when Jaxson

focused on Chase's bottom first, delivering a couple dozen open-handed swats. The loud cracks as hand met flesh filled the bedroom. Emma watched the emotions flit through Chase's eyes as his spanking progressed. She felt comforted by the smoldering sexiness shining back at her, as they remained linked through the hands Chase was squeezing harder with each swat.

Too soon it was Emma's turn. The loud cracks had stopped when she felt Jaxson's warmth near her own trembling body. The first smack filled the room. The sound was much less ominous and she suspected Jax was regulating the strength he was using with her versus the more experienced Chase. Still, after two-dozen spankings to her bare bottom, Emma felt a panic that she wouldn't be able to take much more, yet was desperate not to let Jaxson down.

"That was a decent warm-up. Time for the real thing."

For the first time she saw a flicker of apprehension cross Chase's face which didn't bode well for her already tender ass. In the distance she heard the sound of a metal belt buckle being jostled as Jax prepared the fashion accessory for its secondary job of the day.

Chase jerked his body as the first belt stripe connected with his bare ass. He'd been squeezing her hand lightly, but as the punishment proceeded with a strong, steady rhythm, his intimate grip on her hand tightened.

Each loud crack was an aphrodisiac, driving her deeper into submission. Emma was utterly ashamed that her body was enjoying watching Chase's discipline session. Surely Jaxson would notice her pussy lips covered in cream. She felt a pulsing need emanating from her sexual core and by the time she saw Chase fighting back tears, Emma was ready to beg Jaxson to skip the punishment and take her roughly from behind where she lay instead.

It wasn't in the cards. "I'd better let that be enough, young man, since you have an underwear shoot the day after tomorrow. We wouldn't want you bruised, would we?"

Chase answered with relief, "No, sir. Thank you, sir."

The feel of Jaxson's hand as he caressed her own rounded globes felt outstanding until he addressed her. "Lucky for us, Emma doesn't have the same restriction. I want her to leave here feeling my correction so she can think of tonight while she's on the plane home to Wisconsin. What do you say, Emma?"

Her breath caught in her throat. She was parched and had to croak out a quiet, "Yes, sir." What else was she supposed to say at this juncture?

"Very good girl. You're going to be tempted to reach back with your hands or to move out of position. Chase, please tell your partner in crime here what happens to naughty submissives who get out of position during a punishment."

Chase answered swiftly, "Their punishment is doubled, sir."

"Exactly. Is that an idle threat?"

"No sir. You have doubled my discipline sessions many times because I kept reaching back."

"Thank you, Chase."

Emma's trembling had to be visible to Jaxson because he leaned over and whispered quietly in her ear, all traces of dominance hidden. "What is your safeword, Emma?"

Relief flowed through her. "Puppy, sir."

"Very well. Try your hardest not to use it. I promise not to push you past where I think you can go, but use it if you need to, understood?"

"I will, Jaxson. Thanks."

"You're welcome, sweetheart."

His next words were so harsh in contrast to his loving care just seconds before. "I'm going to light up your bottom now, Emma, and then I'm going to fuck you long and hard."

"Oh, God...."

The first belt stroke left a lick of fire across the center of her bare globes. She had to bite her lip to keep from crying out which didn't bode well at all. Chase's intense gaze warmed her almost as much as the ongoing belting did. She no longer felt guilty for getting turned on when it had been his turn, because he was feral with lust as he relished her expressions as the pain settled into her bottom. She couldn't help the wiggle of her ass as she tried to escape Jaxson's swinging arm, yet she somehow managed to keep her feet on the ground and her hands from reaching back.

"I love how pale your skin is, Emma. It is lighting up to a lovely pink with splotches of redness in places."

She didn't quite know what to say so she whispered a quiet, "Thank you."

The pain grew steadily until she felt on the edge of something. She wasn't sure what it was. As much pain as she was in, she had never been as turned on as she was in that moment.

"Please, Jaxson.... Take me now! I need you inside me so bad."

His satisfied chuckle only made her want him more. He didn't make her ask again. She felt the tip of his erection at the entry to her now sopping wet sex seconds before he lunged forward to impale himself inside her. The tears she had been holding back fell now as he fucked her roughly from behind. She kept her eyes locked with Chase as their fingers were weaved together as he witnessed her falling into her next orgasm. His grin told her she was in trouble again, but she couldn't care less. She was desperate. She'd needed this.

Only when she had come twice did Jax slow his pace, eventually pulling from her pussy without reaching his own release. She felt a failure because he hadn't been able to come while inside her; that was, right up until he pulled himself from her body to step next to her behind Chase. She heard the flick of a cap coming off a jar as Chase's eyes filled with a longing. She risked looking over her shoulder to see Jax smearing lube liberally on Chase's ass. She could only assume he was paying special attention to his puckered back door.

Both men cried out when Jaxson lunged forward to fill Chase's tight hole. He serviced his friend at the same hard, brisk pace he had fucked Emma. Chase's groans turned to grunts as Jaxson bottomed out inside him. All three of them were steeped in the sights and sounds of forbidden sex, taking them each higher. Emma risked Jaxson's wrath by slipping her free hand under her body, flicking her throbbing clit to the same speed of the men's coupling. The squishing sounds were audible to the room and even in his precarious position, Chase grinned, understanding what she was up to.

His staying power was amazing. Jaxson was a damn sex god. It wasn't until he screamed out his own climax that his submissives tipped into their own orgasm.

Chase found his voice first. "Holy fuck. That was amazing."

Jaxson grinned back. "I would say so. What do you think, sweetheart?"

She loved when he used the sweet adornment. "I've had more and better sex in the last twenty-four hours than in all my life combined."

"We're not done with you yet. Let's head to the shower."

CHAPTER 8

*E*mma awoke to the earliest beams of sunlight making their way through the large window. The three of them had made love several times since arriving at the hotel and every inch of her body was filled with an achy satiation. They lay tangled in a mass of arms and legs, not caring who touched whom. The slow, steady breathing of the two men told her they still slept. It gave her a few minutes to evaluate all that had happened.

The most prevalent emotion she felt in the moment was gratitude – grateful she had taken the chance to turn herself over, if even for a few hours, to these two amazing men. She pushed down the sadness of knowing she'd soon say goodbye, surely never to see them again. She may be real, but their lives were larger than life and they would soon return to the spotlight in front of the camera.

Jaxson's voice jarred her out of her thoughts. "You look upset. We didn't hurt you, did we?"

She forced a smile. "No, Jax, you didn't hurt me. At least not in a bad way."

She'd been thinking of their goodbye, but he clearly wasn't

done with her body yet. "Hold that thought. What I have planned this morning will be the most intense yet."

"Oh...." Her pulse quickened on cue.

"You want some breakfast first?"

"That depends.

"On?"

"What you have planned."

"Sorry, kiddo, but you don't get to know yet. Get up and go pee and brush your teeth. We'll be ready for you when you come back." He was still in charge.

She wasn't sure what that meant, but she followed directions.

By the time she returned to the bedroom fifteen minutes later, both men were awake and sporting semi-hard erections as they waited seated on the end of the bed. She went to stand in front of them.

Jax reached out to place his hands on her hips, holding her firmly as he asked, "Emma, we have another question for you. Have you ever had anal sex?"

Her entire body lurched at his blunt question. She rushed to answer, "Oh God... no. I haven't ever... I mean..." she trailed off.

Jax continued calmly, "We want to be your first. We'll take it slow, but only if you are up for it."

She didn't know what to say. Part of her wished Jaxson would keep up his dominant demands, taking what he wanted from her body without asking. That seemed easier than having to give her consent for such a scandalous thing.

Each man reached out to take a hand, linking them together again. She saw raw desire on their faces, making her decision suddenly easy. She was still baffled how they could be so turned on by her body, but as long as they wanted her, she would allow them access to whatever orifice they desired.

Her answer was quiet. "I'm up for it."

They lunged forward as if they'd been on springs. She closed her eyes and let their talented hands roam across her body, bringing her back to life. She marveled that in the short twenty-four hours she'd known them, she could already feel the difference in the men's touch as they pinched, massaged and stroked her to a fever pitch.

"Chase, on your back." The order was brusque and the blond man rushed to comply, lying in the middle of the bed, nursing his rigid cock slowly in his left hand to keep his need at bay.

"Emma, crawl on top. Take his hard cock in your pussy, baby."

He didn't need to tell her twice. She moved quickly to comply, lining up the blunt head of Chase's erection with her wet core and slowly lowering herself until he filled her.

Jaxson continued to direct them. "Very good. Fuck, it looks hot from back here. Lean forward now, sweetheart and kiss him. Then I want you to start fucking yourself slowly while I take things to the next level."

Emma complied, excitement coursing through her body as she contemplated what the next level might be. She didn't have to wait long as a cold, wet finger grazed her rosebud, massaging her private hole intimately. She tried not to think about the sight she made or the fact she wasn't one of those women who had professional waxes to remove unsightly hair. No. She was real and raw and if the low groans from Jaxson were any indication, she was exactly what he wanted.

She panicked briefly when he breeched her tight ring, pushing first one and then two fingers inside her. It didn't hurt, but the fullness was uncomfortable and got worse when he began scissoring his fingers to stretch her puckered hole.

"Oh God, Jaxson!"

Luckily for her, he didn't interpret her exclamation as a request to stop. Instead, he doubled his efforts, slipping a third finger in her ass and then began pumping in and out, emulating what she suspected his cock would be doing as soon as he had her body primed and ready. She had been so distracted she'd forgotten to raise herself up and down, but Chase seemed to understand, grabbing her hips in his grip as he began lifting his ass off the bed to slam his tool deep into her sloppy pussy. He kept up the pace until she was begging to come.

"Please... sir... I need to... can I... oh God... can I come?" She wailed.

Instead of granting permission, Jax removed his fingers completely, reaching for a nearby towel.

She felt the weight of Jax joining them on the bed. Chase was watching her through lust filled eyes as she waited to have her virgin ass taken. The moment felt momentous.

Jaxson stroked the tip of his manhood through the lube, bringing the sensitive skin around her puckered hole alive with need. She kept waiting for the breach, but it didn't come. The men strummed her higher and higher until she felt ready to explode.

She didn't know what he was waiting for until he grunted, "Ask for it, Emma. Tell me what you want."

Damn him. Why did he keep doing this to her? Why couldn't he just take her? She'd already given her consent. She felt her face flushing with embarrassment as Chase watched her with hooded eyes beneath her. She tried to shut him out, but Chase wouldn't allow it.

"Eyes on me, Emma. We're waiting. Ask for what you need, sweetheart."

"Why?" It was a whisper.

"Because it pleases us."

His answer was so simple yet persuasive. She wanted to do anything and everything to please these men who had changed her life forever.

The words fell from her lips. "Please, Jaxson. Take me in the ass. I want you to fuck my virgin hole."

"Christ, Emma. That's so hot."

Despite the urgency in his voice, he pressed forward slowly. The pressure on her tight ring was intense as it denied the over-sized intruder access. Finally, he pressed forward and she felt the head of his cock pop into her orifice, dragging a surprised cry from her lungs. She was relieved when both men held still, allowing her body time to grow accustomed to the dual stretching. They all panted heavily with pent up desire until Jaxson began his slow trek deeper into her tight channel.

She couldn't say it hurt, but it sure as hell felt weird. With each inch he claimed, her body became more full. The groan from Chase beneath her told her he could now feel Jaxson's cock rubbing him through the thin layer of flesh separating the men's appendages.

Jax took his time, pushing in and out slowly until he was sure he had her stretched and lubed. The fullness turned to a burning sensation, feeling both amazing and painful at the same time. She hadn't experienced anything like it, and let the foreign feelings consume her.

Chase had remained rather still, letting Jaxson have his turn with her body, but when Jax barked his next order of "It's time!" It was as if the starting gun had been shot to begin a race. Both men moved in concert, pulling out and pushing back inside her two tight holes like pistons in a running motor. The friction of their cocks rubbing against each other as they plunged in and out of her heated them all to a boiling point. This naughty orgy would not be lasting much longer.

She was so close to coming when Jax broke rhythm to hold back one stroke until he could plunge inside her ass at the exact moment Chase filled her pussy next. Being filled completely by two huge cocks together was the final straw, pushing her into the most intense orgasm of her life, made better by the feel of both men depositing their heavy loads of cum deep inside her body.

They remained locked together for a long minute, catching their breath until Jaxson began to relax, placing his weight on Emma and sandwiching her between them. It was Chase who complained.

"What the hell are you trying to do, suffocate me down here man?" He said it with a relaxed grin.

"Give me a break, will ya? I'm not ready to pull out yet."

Chase agreed. "I hear that." He leaned up to capture her lips in a kiss. Their tongues tangled until she felt Jaxson's now softening shaft slip from her body, leaving behind a wet trail across her ass.

He pulled her to her side and all three of them snuggled together, recovering from the best sex of her life.

* * *

THEY HAD OFFERED to see her all the way to the airport, but she'd turned them down. It would be bad enough saying goodbye to them here at the hotel. She didn't want to make a fool of herself crying at the airport. The threesome was quiet as they took the elevator to the lobby. Both men brushed close, refusing to release her yet.

They wrestled her luggage to the door where the same livery driver was waiting, this time to take her to Charles de Gaulle for her flight home. Last week she'd been getting homesick, ready to see family. Today, she wished she could stay indefinitely, yet she knew part of what had made their time together so magical was the expiration date on the tryst. They'd entered this knowing their time would be short. She couldn't complain about the rules now.

Chase hugged her first, pulling her into an open mouth kiss full of a promise he couldn't fulfill. She fought back her tears as he smiled softly, releasing her to his friend.

Jaxson held her too, but his kiss was tender, almost reverent. When their lips parted, she felt the hot tears streaming down her cheeks, as he seemed to look into her soul. He swiped at her tears with the pads of his thumbs, a wan smile on his lips as if he was trying to convince them both to cheer up. "I'm glad we met you,

Emma...." His face registered his shock. "Fuck... I don't even know your last name."

Emma smiled through her growing tears. "Does it matter?"

The sorrow she saw reflected back at her was surprising. "I guess not. We're gonna miss you. Safe travels, sweetheart."

"You too, Jaxson."

He grinned. "That's sir to you."

She grinned through her tears, "Yes, sir."

The next few minutes moved in a strange slow motion. Emma's ears were ringing as her heart contracted with a physical ache as she watched the two men who'd changed her life forever growing smaller as the car pulled out into the busy Parisan traffic. She raised her hand to wave, knowing they couldn't see it through the tinted windows.

The driver jarred her from her trance. "Looks like it's difficult saying goodbye. How long until you see them again?"

The dam holding back her tears broke, sobs wracking her body as she cried out her answer. "Never!"

CHAPTER 9

*J*t might only be two weeks into the summer semester, but Emma already felt the pressure growing from her heavy grad school schedule. The only good thing about her grueling work lineup was that it left precious little time for her to wallow in regret over having said goodbye to the two extraordinary men who'd made her a woman in France. At times, it felt like it had been one big dream.

She only had one regret, which grew stronger with each passing day. Why hadn't she given them her last name and her phone number that final morning? Even as she thought it, she knew it wouldn't have mattered. Emma was a fool to entertain the idea that they might have wanted to stay in touch. Her brain knew the swift split was best, but her heart hurt at the thought of never seeing Chase or Jaxson again.

Finding their last names had been easy. A few minutes on Google and she had enough information to keep her busy reading for hours. They weren't just models–they were A-list models, in demand for top-end ad campaigns around the globe. Her investigation had dug up more than just their professional portfolio. The Internet was full of candid pictures of Jax and

Chase at back-stage parties, fundraisers and even movie premiers. They were regularly photographed with musicians, movie stars and politicians who traveled in the circles of the rich and famous.

Emma was grateful she hadn't known just how famous they were when they'd been together. Now, knowing who they really were, she treasured their intimate time spent together even more knowing she'd seen a side to the extraordinary men the cameras never got to see. She was proud that they'd trusted her enough to show her the real them.

"Emma! I'm back!" She was jarred out of her memories by the voice of a person she had hoped would never come searching for her. She glanced up to see Bianca sauntering towards her, dressed as if she were headed to a fashion show instead of an Econ 101 class. She was surrounded by two other Barbie doll wanna-be's who appeared to be hanging on her every word. Emma had to fight down the giggle when she realized how silly Bianca looked.

Not wanting to engage, Emma moved around her to continue on to the lecture hall where class was to begin in ten minutes.

"Hello? How rude! If you won't talk to me as a friend, you can at least tell me what assignments I've missed so I can get caught up."

Emma stopped in her tracks. Surely Bianca wasn't that stupid.

She turned to address her previous travel companion. "You can't be serious. It's summer. We cover a chapter per class. You've missed four chapters already. Drop the class."

"No way. I need this as a pre-req for a class in the fall."

Anger flared. "Then I guess you should have come home sooner instead of gallivanting around Europe on the back of Marrrio with an R's moped."

"It was a Vespa," she whined as if that made a difference.

Emma chuckled at Bianca's childish behavior. "Fine, suit your-self. Come to class, but don't expect anything special from me. You'll do the work like everyone else."

Anger flashed across Bianca's pinched face. "What's wrong with you? You seem different... like a total bitch."

Emma didn't deny it. She had changed. "I am different, but you'd better be careful about calling your professor names. I might have to take points off on your next test to dock you."

One of Bianca's fan club turned her nose up, hurling what she thought was an insult. "Someone needs to get laid. Wait–girls like you can't get a guy, can you? Maybe that's your problem."

In that moment, Emma's heart ached for Chase and Jaxson and strangely, it wasn't so she could flaunt them in front of these bitches. It wasn't even for the sex... okay it wasn't *only* for the sex.

In the two weeks since they'd said farewell, Emma had figured out what she missed the most was how they made her feel when they were together. As if she were a queen, worthy of their attention. She longed to be the center of someone's attention as she'd been with not just one, but both men.

No, she couldn't share that with Bianca. There was no point since the bitch would never believe her anyway.

A tense thirty seconds passed in the hall as the women squared off. Emma refused to fight at their level, instead choosing to walk around them to proceed to the lecture hall.

She was five minutes into her lecture when Bianca and her entourage finally strolled in late, taking a seat towards the front of the room, causing a commotion as all of the students present stopped to watch the show they were putting on with their strutting. Emma was in no mood to put up with Bianca's childish behavior.

"How thoughtful of you to join us two weeks late, Miss Branson. I see you brought friends who aren't even registered as students for the class. You hoping they'll be able to help you catch up?"

Bianca appeared shocked to be called out in front of the entire lecture hall of fifty plus students. Seeing her face reminded Emma of how much she had changed since meeting the men. She was so much calmer now. Confident. Not willing to put up with immature bullshit.

Bianca spewed back hurtful words. "At least I have friends. You're gonna end up alone in life, you know that Emma?"

Direct hit. It was Emma's number one fear. A deep sadness settled in as she realized the amazing men she'd allowed to see the real her didn't even know her last name. Their friendship was an illusion. She hated Bianca for saying the words she hated to hear the most... she was alone while they were still in Paris rubbing shoulders with the rich and famous. The worst part was she already knew no man would ever be able to compete with the memories of two extraordinary men who swept her off her feet, ruining her for all men going forward.

"Why are you letting her get to you, sweetheart? You should tell her the truth. That you've found not one but two men to spend your time with?"

Emma was losing her mind. There was no other explanation for hearing Jaxson's voice nearby. She'd officially missed them so much she was hallucinating now. The only clue that perhaps it wasn't a figment of her imagination was the look of jealous shock on Bianca's face.

Time stood still. They could hear a pin drop, the huge lecture hall was so silent. She didn't dare turn towards the voice because then she'd have to admit she'd imagined Jax was there. They visited her in her dreams, but she was losing it if she was imagining them in the middle of class.

It wasn't until strong arms hugged her from behind, pulling her back against a muscular chest that she'd recognize anywhere that she allowed hope to take hold. He whispered into her ear. "Hi, baby. We missed you."

"Jaxson." His name escaped her lips like a prayer as Chase stepped in front of her, a wide grin on his tanned face.

"Emma." His voice held a soulful longing as his eyes danced with desire.

"Chase." She whispered, still afraid to scare her dream away. Her heart thumped in her chest.

He moved forward, hugging her and Jax, sandwiching her between them as they had so often while they were together.

"How?" She was once again incapable of forming full sentences.

"You're the only Emma grad student TA in Econ at the University of Wisconsin."

She shook her head lightly, hoping to clear the cobwebs from her brain. "But why?"

This time the men answered in unison. "Because we missed you."

"But..."

As usual Jaxson took control of the situation, stepping out from behind her, leaving Emma in Chase's embrace to address the group of students watching with interest. "Your professor has another engagement she must attend so class is dismissed for today. Come back for the next class on Friday."

Most of the class sprang to their feet, thrilled to get the summer morning back, but Bianca and her friends sat sulking. When the lecture hall was relatively empty, Bianca stood. "This is an amazing joke, Emma. I'm surprised you'd spend money to hire these guys to pretend to be into you."

It was Jaxson who answered. "I think you're the joke. We took the next month off to try to convince Emma to go on tour with us this fall."

He glanced back at Emma, suddenly looking vulnerable. As if he didn't know how much she'd missed him since they'd parted two weeks before.

"Right. And I'm sure you're selling the Brooklyn Bridge next." Bianca wasn't buying it. "Emma couldn't get even one of you guys in a million years."

Jaxson countered her quickly. "You're right. She didn't get one of us." He paused for effect "We're a package deal and Emma got us both. We're a trio." Bianca wilted under Jaxson's dominant stare. "We couldn't forget about her after she left. The time she spent in our bed in Paris was amazing." When Bianca still looked skeptical, he added. "Jaxson Davidson and Chase Cartwright. Google us, sweetheart." Sarcasm dripped with his term of endearment this time.

Bianca's laugh died when Jaxson turned to take Emma in his arms and place a sexy kiss on her lips. She melted into him and went like a wet noodle when he handed off her body to a waiting Chase who claimed his own X-rated kiss.

By the time they separated, Emma caught the sour look on Bianca's face as she glanced up from her tablet having Googled the men. Insane jealousy turned the attractive co-ed to a shrew. She looked as if she might be sick as she realized who the men were.

Jax moved in to press his hard body against Emma's back, the feel of his semi-hard erection poking her as the three of them held each other close, enjoying the feel of being together again. Relief they had sought her out flooded through Emma.

Jaxson took control. "Let's get out of here. We have a lot to talk to you about, baby."

"Yes, sir."

CHAPTER 10

JAXSON'S JOURNEY

*J*axson's hands trembled as he pulled Emma into his arms. He breathed in the fresh apple smell of her shampoo as he tucked her against his body. Chase crowded at her back, sandwiching her between them.

His body relaxed – finally.

In the weeks since they'd let Emma walk out of their lives, Jaxson had been carrying a tension that no amount of rest or exercise had been able to relieve. He'd tried several over-the-counter pain relievers in an attempt to medicate the empty feeling away while the normally happy-go-lucky Chase had turned into a sour companion.

It hadn't been easy for the confident men to come to terms with the fact that they couldn't stop thinking about their sexy co-ed. It took even longer to admit to themselves and each other that they weren't going to be happy until they did something about it.

Jaxson was under no delusion. The chances of the three of them turning their summer fling into any kind of relationship that had sticking power were slim. Still, they had unfinished business with the curvy brunette currently crying on his shoulder and he planned on staying in Wisconsin long enough to understand exactly what that meant.

The sound of titters of laughter broke the moment, reminding him they were still in a public location. He hoped to lay low under the radar for a few weeks and getting their pictures plastered on the front page of the student newspaper wasn't a good way to make that happen.

"We need to move somewhere more private."

Emma's answer was muffled by the shirt she clung to as if she were afraid he'd disappear like a mirage. "We should go back to my house."

Chase groaned in pain. "I won't make it that long. Somewhere closer?"

"Well... I guess... my office, but it's small."

Jax's neglected cock made the decision for him. "Lead the way."

They shuffled their way through the winding hallways, stopping when they had a modicum of privacy to steal a kiss or grope a body part. When Emma's hands shook too much to unlock her office door, Jax took the key and wrestled the old wood open.

Emma had exaggerated when she'd called the space small. It was a tiny cubbyhole of a teacher's assistant office, but it would do for a quickie.

The men made fast work of tugging at her clothes, longing to touch bare skin. Jax stretched his leg back to kick the door closed.

The slam of the heavy wood acted as a starter's whistle in a race. Jaxson divested Emma of her sundress while Chase pulled the small desk to the center of the windowless room, pushing the paperwork on top to the floor.

"Christ, Emma, we've missed you." Jaxson's lips found their way to the tender juncture where neck met shoulder. His teeth nicked her as he sucked, hoping to leave his mark as he hugged her closer. He worked the clasp of her lacy bra with ease, exposing her breasts to the men.

They worked in unison to lean her back onto the desk, her

hips at the edge. Chase's mouth found her right nipple as Jax hooked his fingers into the waist of her panties pulling them down her long, bare legs. An uncontrolled shiver shook Emma's body. He suspected it was due to a combination of sexual excitement and the air conditioning set too low for her naked body.

Chase's long hair tickled her chest. Man, he'd missed the sound of her playful giggle as he paid homage to her breasts with his sucking mouth and squeezing hands.

Jax stepped back and admired his lovers starting their fun without him as he shucked off his own clothes. Emma watched Jax strip as she held Chase tight to her chest. Their eyes connected just before she dropped her heated glare to his boxer briefs. She licked her lips as anticipation grew.

"Jaxson..." His name was her plea for more.

"Emma." He was their Dom. He should slow things down. Make this moment last, but the sound of students shuffling down the hall outside the door reminded him this might not be the best place for seduction. No. A red-hot fucking is what was called for and by-God he was gonna deliver it.

His briefs hit the floor, springing his hardness free. He instructed Chase, "Drop your pants, Chase. Let's see that fat boner of yours."

Chase grinned as he stood, his lips glistening with lingering wetness from his feast at her breast. Jaxson and Emma froze, admiring Chase's speedy strip tease. He had to hide his smile at Emma's awe-filled expression as she took in the view of their lover's thick cock. Surprised relief coursed through Jax as he realized the sight of the hardness turned him on.

Chase and Jax had done something they had not done in a while after Emma left them weeks ago in Paris. When it was clear they both missed her more than they wanted to admit, they'd tried playing just the two of them, hoping to recapture some of the lost intimacy.

Chase had been on his knees anxious to accept Jaxson's cock in his mouth or tight ass many times over the year since they'd become lovers. But like the past, they just couldn't capture the same level of intimacy alone that they could when they had a submissive woman between them. Only recently was Jax coming to terms with the fact that what had started as a fun experimentation at an after-party full of naked women was turning into a long-term life choice.

Sex with a hot woman was good. Sex with Chase was okay. Sex with a sexy woman and Chase together was awesome.

But, sex with Chase and Emma together had been fucking life changing. That was the only way he could describe it and his own emotions honestly baffled him. The men had fucked women more beautiful than their Emma. Ladies with bigger breasts, flatter tummies, or longer legs. It had taken the time apart from her for Jax to start to piece together what was the real magnet pulling him to Madison, Wisconsin.

Emma was genuine, and in his life, that was a rare gift.

The joy on her face in that moment was pure. She laid bare before them in every sense of the word. Her trust humbled him.

Emma reached out to stroke Chase's cock until pre-cum glistened on the tip. Jaxson stepped closer so Emma's other free hand could encircle his own hardness. Her grip on his cock was tight as she stroked both men in unison, laid prone on her back, spread out like a feast on her small desk.

Jaxson felt Chase's heated gaze. He glanced up to see longing in his friend's eyes. The men leaned in wordlessly, joining their lips together reverently at first until the heat of the moment consumed them. Tongues tangled. The same tongues that had tried to recapture the intimacy and failed when alone. It truly took Emma between them to complete the electric circuit, lighting up all three lovers.

Jax dominated Chase's open mouth, weaving his fingers through his shoulder length-hair and yanking hard enough to elicit a groan of surrender. Only his approaching orgasm could force him to separate. He wasn't ready to come yet. He would do that buried inside the panting co-ed stroking his cock.

"Chase–in her mouth. I get her pussy." His instructions were abrupt. The men worked in unison to center their co-ed's body across her perfect-sized desk. Her legs bent at the knee, her feet on the edge of the table, spreading herself wide open for the taking. As if it had been designed as a sex-aide, Emma's head hung over the other end of the furniture, her neck stretching back so her head was inverted, her mouth at the perfect height to receive Chase's appendage. Jax enjoyed the first moments of Chase's domination of her throat. The gagging as he thrust deep added the perfect soundtrack to the scene.

He waited until his lovers were consumed with each other completely before he stepped closer and thrust his shaft balls-deep into her dripping core in one stroke. He knew from experience how wonderful Emma's strangled cry felt as her throat contracted around Chase's rod.

"Don't you dare come yet, Chase. We come together."

His friend shot him a defiant look that quickly turned to pain from the strain of holding off his eruption. Jax didn't tell him that he wouldn't have long to wait as his own cum was close to boiling over. Bodies slapped together hard and fast as the men reclaimed Emma as their own. Chase reached down to massage her mounds just as Jax grabbed her hips and moved into high gear, pistoning her as he chased his orgasm.

He held off as long as he could, but was eventually forced to cry out "Now!" as he felt the jism spurting into her body. Emma's body hugged him as she rode out the waves of ecstasy. When she started to choke on the volume of cum Chase had deposited in her mouth, he pulled out to shoot the last spurt onto her pebbled nipple.

For a full minute the only sound in the tiny room was the labored breathing of all three occupants as they recovered from their exertion. As his heart rate returned to normal, the sounds of the students walking by the office just feet away returned.

They moved in slow motion, helping Emma to her feet and embracing again before they all rummaged around the floor for their strewn-off clothes.

They were all the way out to the parking lot before Emma seemed to come out of her trance to ask, "Where are we going?"

Jax opened the door to the Ford truck they'd rented, holding it open for Emma to climb in. "Your place, of course."

"But... I live with roommates... in an old house."

"Do you have a bed?"

"Yes."

"What size?"

"Queen."

He grinned. "Sounds perfect."

She turned to get into the truck, needing his help to climb in. He enjoyed the view of her delicious ass struggling to settle in. Only once they were pulling out of the lot did she ask, "Why did you guys rent a truck?"

Chase answered by turning to pull her into his lap, his hands roaming her body. "We asked for anything that had a bench seat so we could ravage you as we travel."

It was all Jax could do to pay attention to the road with the distraction of Emma and Chase getting started on their next session only inches away. Luckily, Emma's house was only a few blocks off-campus.

* * *

"I DON'T THINK this is a very good idea." Emma remained planted in the truck, despite the fact the men had piled out and were waiting for her impatiently.

Jax suspected she'd forgotten that he was the one that would make the call on where they stayed. "Chase, grab our bags. Emma, give me your hand. We're going inside."

The pupils in her beautiful lavender eyes dilated and for a brief moment he thought she might challenge him. Her soft "Yes, sir" went straight to his cock, filling it in preparation for their next tryst.

The house was an old two-story brick brownstone that looked like it'd been housing college students since the beginning of time. It stopped just short of being described as run-down. Tired was the word that came to Jaxson as they climbed the worn steps to cross over the large old-fashioned porch, swing and all. The front door stuck as if it wanted to refuse entry and only Emma's left hip applied in a swift push finally nudged it forward.

The front room was a collage of worn, mismatched furniture. Jaxson's eyes fixated on the out-of-place modern love-seat in the middle of the room facing the entertainment center. The back of the couch was the perfect height to lay Chase and Emma across to apply his leather belt as they squirmed and whimpered. He shook his head to clear the sexual daydream as he followed Emma through a dining room with a heavy wood dining table that would seat eight for dinner; that is if it weren't full of papers, computers and what looked like the beginning of a class project.

Just before they went through the swinging door to the kitchen the sounds of sex hit his ears. He reached out to stop Emma from proceeding just before she pushed open the door. The three of them huddled together silently to listen to the rhythmic clapping of what sounded like wood on wood coming from the other side of the door. It might have sounded like someone building something were it not for the filthy rant accompanying the banging.

"Oh God, Ryan. That's it. Harder. I like it hard."

"I know you do, you little slut."

"Shit, I love it when you call me your little slut. Ride me."

A loud crack followed by a wailing howl came next. "Ouch.

What was that for?" The woman on the receiving end of the spank complained.

"No reason. I just love to see my handprint on your ass is all."

Thirty seconds more of hot-and-heavy sex culminated in the couple crying out as they came together. "Shit, Court. Come, baby."

Jaxson knew he was being a dick, but he only waited a few seconds before pushing through the door. The copulating couple didn't see them at first, but when they did, the half-naked woman squeaked as she scrambled to pull on her disheveled clothes while the bearded man looked mildly amused at literally being caught with his pants around his ankles.

Jaxson's sixth sense alarm bells went off when the guy looked Emma up and down as if she were a juicy steak even while another woman's pussy cream dripped from his unprotected cock. Jaxson's facial expression must have told the guy to back-the-fuck-up because his jovial smile waned when he noticed Jaxson staring him down.

Emma tried to smooth things over. "Sorry, Courtney. I didn't know you and Ryan would be home."

Courtney's face was a bright pink, he presumed from embarrassment. "Aren't you supposed to be teaching a class?" She accused, before continuing. "Who the hell are you guys?"

That she had to ask surprised him. Not because she should have recognized them, which she really should have. He tried not to feel disappointed that Emma clearly hadn't told her roommates about meeting the men in Paris.

When Emma failed to introduce them, Jaxson took charge. Placing his arm around her shoulders to pull her against his side. "I'm Jax. I'm with Emma."

"With Emma? As in *with* Emma?" He wasn't sure why the redhead acted so surprised. Well if she was shocked that he was with her roommate, he was about to blow her mind.

"Most definitely *with* Emma. And this is our lover, Chase." As if they'd choreographed it, Chase moved in to wrap his arm around Emma's waist, linking the three of them together, their lovely grad student sandwiched between them.

Jaxson wanted to smack the grin off the bitch's face. "That's a good one, Emma. Who are these guys, really? You haven't dated anyone since Bob last year and let's face it, these guys are way out of your league."

Jaxson was ready to bitch-slap her for dissing Emma, but Chase had a better idea as he pulled Emma into his arms, capturing her with a searing kiss. She melted into his arms while Jaxson pressed his chest against her back, slipping his hands around her to squeeze her heavy breasts through her sundress while sucking on her neck. Only when her legs started to collapse like they were made with Jell-O did Jaxson take charge and scoop her up into his arms.

"Which way to your room, sweetheart?"

"Upstairs. Top floor." She answered breathlessly.

Leave it to Chase to know the perfect thing to say on their way out of the kitchen towards the back stairs. "If you have any doubts, feel free to listen in. We can be pretty loud when we all three come at the same time."

Jaxson got to the second floor landing and Emma struggled to be put down. "I'm too heavy!"

He pinned her with a stare that stopped her from continuing. "I know it's been a few weeks, but the rules haven't changed. What did I tell you would happen if you put yourself down, Emma?"

Fear mixed with desire flickered through her violet eyes. Ah yes, his little sub had missed the feel of his belt. He'd be happy to remedy that soon. "Well?" he prompted.

"You said... I mean... I should never put myself down."

"Yes, and?"

"That I need to believe I'm beautiful."

"Do you? Believe you're beautiful?"

"I do when you look at me like that." It was almost a whisper.

"That's better. Next time, I'll remind you with my belt."

"Oh God."

He grinned. "Who am I kidding? You're gonna feel my belt no matter what. The only question is whether you hate it or love it."

Chase was urging them to keep pressing forward. "All of this talk of belts is making me hot. Which room is yours?"

Emma nodded towards the next set of stairs at the end of the hall. "My room is the attic. We need to go up another flight."

Chase went ahead of them. The room was spacious, but darker than the rest of the house with only one window in the eave of the roof. A large work desk was pushed next to the window to take advantage of the natural light. The walls were lined with shelves, filled with books, CD's, movies, and knick-knacks. A tall armoire stood open, overflowing with clothes, shoes and purses.

Emma was wiggling in his arms, trying to escape. Her eyes kept darting towards the large bulletin board near her desk. He grinned as he saw she'd made a makeshift shrine to the men who had changed her life in Paris. Dozen's of magazine ads and photos from the Internet decorated every inch of the board.

He looked down at the embarrassed woman in his arms. She offered a simple explanation. "I missed you."

"We missed you too, baby. That's why we're here."

The large bed in the center of the room was a welcome sight. He couldn't wait to get his lovers naked again. He planned on spending many hours playing in this bed.

He stepped closer and dropped Emma into the middle, letting her bounce with a giggle as Chase pounced on her. Jaxson took his time undressing, watching as Emma and Chase started without him. He'd missed this. He'd missed watching his lovers almost as much as he'd missed participating. He'd always been a voyeur, enjoying watching sexy scenes. Watching Chase and Emma could turn into an addiction. He let his mind dream and his heart hope as he watched his lovers.

Meeting Emma had him thinking about what was going to

come after his modeling career wound down in a few years. There was a time when he'd thought he wanted to move behind the camera, but the more time he'd spent in the modeling industry, the less attractive that sounded. He was looking forward to taking the rest of the summer off to try to get his head on straight.

His cock filled at the sight of Chase's muscular bare ass. Christ, he loved marking that ass almost as much as he loved fucking it. In the weeks since Emma had left them in Paris, he'd had to do some soul searching. He'd been surprised at what he'd discovered.

First, he'd come to terms with the fact that he was falling in love with his best friend. Outsiders might call them gay, but they'd be wrong. It would honestly be easier if it could be that simple. No. They were soul mates. Friends. Lovers. Sharers. He had also come to terms that the only thing better than being with Chase was being with both Chase and Emma together.

As if they'd suddenly realized he hadn't joined them yet, the action in the bed stopped and four eyes turned his way, looking at him expectantly. He was their leader and he would live up to that honor.

"Chase, get the lube from your duffle." His instructions were stern, bringing a smolder to Chase's gaze.

"Yes, sir."

And just like that they were in scene. Chase scrambled for the lube, returning to the bed with not only the tube, but also an armful of sex toys.

Jaxson slipped farther into his dominant role. "Chase, hand the lube to Emma then get on the bed on your hands and knees."

Chase looked confused, but he followed directions. Jaxson watched the look on her face as he gave their little subby her instructions. "Squeeze some lube on your fingers, Emma, and then I want you to prepare Chase's tight little rosebud for my cock. I'm gonna fuck him while he fucks you."

In that moment Jaxson realized that lust had a distinctive smell. He wished he could bottle the scent and sell it because he was sure people around the globe would love to steep themselves in the smell of longing permeating the air.

Emma sat frozen, unsure how to proceed. Ironically, it was Chase who helped her by holding out the now open bottle of lube to pour it liberally on her fingers. He had brought a small towel and handed it to her. He then crawled in front of her, stuck his ass up, his cheek down on his sheet and his legs spread wide to expose his waxed bottom.

"Touch him Emma. Rub circles around his tight hole. Spread the lube around a bit."

As if she were in a trance, Emma reached out tentatively, barely making contact with Chase's most private body part. A low groan escaped from their lover when she began to run up and down the crevasse of his ass. It was clear to Jax she had no intention of penetrating Chase.

"That's it, sweetheart. Now stick a finger inside. Push it all the way in and leave it in there."

She looked back for confirmation she had heard him correctly so he nodded sharply. It took her a full minute of caressing before her first knuckle disappeared inside Chase's anus. Her finger was tiny compared to the cock that would be there soon.

"Good girl. Now two fingers." He was pushing her out of her comfort zone. Her shy tentativeness was a huge turn-on for the Dom.

Chase's moans helped spur her forward and within a few seconds she had slipped two fingers into his stretching channel. Jaxson's own balls tightened with desire at the sight of Chase's cock and balls swinging between his spread legs as Emma's manicured fingers shoved deep inside him.

"You're doing great, Emma. Move your fingers in and out." When she froze, he commanded her. "Now. Fuck him."

She obeyed immediately, thrusting her fingers in and out, a sloppy slurping sound enhancing the ambiance as Chase squeezed his ass tight around the slim intruders.

"Now take your left hand and cup his balls. Squeeze them. Massage them while you finger fuck him."

Jaxson wasn't sure which one of his lovers was breathing heavier as their session unfolded. Emma had kneeled up and was leaning over Chase's body to gain better leverage. As she'd repositioned, she'd unconsciously spread her own legs, exposing her glistening pussy to her Dom.

Jaxson was pleased she'd been keeping her snatch shaved and he couldn't wait to glide his tongue through that sweet slit of hers. That would have to wait until later. They'd had enough foreplay. It was time to fuck.

"Take your fingers out, Emma, and wipe them on the towel. Then take Chase's spot. On your hands and knees—nice and wide."

She scrambled to accomplish her task, moving erratically in her excitement. Like a natural, she positioned herself perfectly. Chase didn't need instructions. He lined up behind her, placing the tip of his shaft at her entrance and held there, waiting for instructions like a good submissive.

Jaxson stepped close to the bed, happy it was the perfect height to service the hole in front of him. Both he and Chase were leaning forward. The trio fit together like a perfectly designed puzzle. Jax bit Chase's neck, trying to hold off penetration as long as possible.

He grabbed his partner's hips, and cried out "now" just as he thrust his cock into Chase's tight channel. Jax adored the sexy grunt Chase made each time he took a cock and today was no different. Jaxson's rod was squeezed like a vice until he slowly pulled out.

The second his bottom was empty, Chase thrust his pelvis forward, dipping his own penis into the very wet pussy in front of him. Only when he had pulled out did Jax thrust forward again. The men worked in unison, building speed until their naughty dance had all three lovers on the edge of the cliff, ready to free fall into a blissful vortex.

It was the sight of tears of joy streaming down Emma's turned cheek as she received her pleasure that tipped Jaxson into his climax. With a loud grunt he emptied the contents of his balls deep into Chase's bowels. Within seconds, Chase did the same buried deep inside Emma. She was the last to tip into her orgasm with a shriek.

A full minute later, Jax had recovered enough to plop the three of them over onto their sides, somehow managing to keep his softening shaft inside his lover.

Chase's voice was already fading as he urged, "I vote for a nap."

Emma giggled, snuggled into the men's arms. "I second that vote."

CHAPTER 11

"Seriously, guys. I need to go to sleep now. I can't miss class again tomorrow. I'm gonna get fired."

Jax held her tighter as he nibbled her ear. "You've figured out our plan. If we can't convince you to come on the road with us, we've decided to resort to getting you kicked out."

He was only half kidding.

"So what exactly would I do if I went on the road with you? Hang out in the hotel room every day?"

"Not at all. You could come on set or go shopping. And don't forget, we need someone to manage our riches. You'd be perfect for the job."

"But what about my masters degree? I've already started and I don't want to be a quitter."

"You can finish with on-line classes from anywhere in the world. Next objection?"

They'd been through this argument many times. Jaxson could see progress. In the beginning she had refused to even consider leaving Wisconsin with them when they left in two weeks. He suspected she was finally giving a future with the men some serious thought.

Ironically, Jax had expected to become restless with this much time off, but between the marathon sexcapades, long runs along Lake Mendota, and binge drinking and eating, he'd accomplished the near impossible.

He had truly relaxed.

The thought of going back to the grind of their modeling schedule stressed him, but the thought of doing it without Emma with them downright depressed him. He had halfway expected to have her worked out of his system by now. He had never been known for long-term relationships. In fact, other than his long-standing friendship and now quasi-relationship with Chase, he'd never felt this way before.

The two weeks they'd spent in Madison had been some of the best of his life. It was the first time in his adult life he'd given himself permission to just be.

Before they'd come, he'd made reservations for a suite at the best hotel in town, expecting to treat Emma to a month of luxury. Instead, she'd convinced them they'd have a better chance of remaining anonymous by staying with her at her house just off campus.

He hated to admit it, but she'd been right.

For years they'd been treated like celebrities everywhere they went and while being rich and famous certainly had its perks, he hadn't realized how much he missed just being able to fade into the crowd. The men had lost touch with reality and their time in Wisconsin was restoring an equilibrium he hadn't even known was out of whack.

The fact that Emma not only understood that, but refused to capitalize on the men's fame in any way put her in uncharted territory for Jax. Only through distance could he see that the people he'd been surrounded by for the last few years had all wanted something from him. Money. Fame. Connections.

Emma wanted none of those things. She simply wanted him.

The real him, and he hadn't known how important that was until it happened.

Now that they'd passed the halfway mark of their month-long vacation, Jax found himself analyzing his life in a way he hadn't in years. At twenty-six years old, he found himself examining how many more years he had left in his modeling career. The fact that he had started to dread going back on the road was revealing.

Unaware of Jaxson's inner conflict, Chase rolled over to reach for the remote control from the nightstand. When the men had found Emma had no television they'd gone out and purchased a big-ass smart TV that took up a whole section of the attic. They'd spent hours curled up watching movie after movie, taking intermissions for sex, sleep and food. As nice as the break had been, he found the tension returning in small increments with each day they marked off on the calendar.

Happy-go-lucky Chase didn't seem to suffer from the same self-awareness issues.

While Jaxson tried to distract himself on his iPad, Emma and Chase wrestled for control over the remote. Chase tickled their lover and she broke into a fit of giggles, sending a jolt of longing through Jax.

He didn't want this to end.

Hours later, Jaxson lay awake. His two lovers were each snuggled close on either side of him, their hands intertwined on his chest, linking the three together even in sleep. His mind wouldn't shut off and he hated it. He spent hours looking at his choices from every possible angle. In the end, he knew what he needed to do. He just hoped Emma would come around.

* * *

BRIGHT LIGHT SHINING in through the one window in the attic woke Jaxson many hours later. He hadn't looked at the clock yet, but knew by the angle of the sun it had to be almost noon. Emma would be done with her classes soon. He cracked an eye to see Chase sitting up in bed next to him, his body propped up with pillows, an X-box controller in his hand.

"It's about time you woke up. I never thought I'd say this, but I'm actually getting sick of video games."

"I know what you mean. It's been a long time since I've been able to sleep until I woke up without an alarm."

Chase flipped off the TV and threw down the controller to turn his attention to his full-time friend and part-time Dom and lover.

"Emma's gone. So talk to me. What's bothering you?"

The men had known each other way too long to pretend there was nothing wrong. He just didn't know if he was ready to talk about it yet.

Chase waited patiently until the uncomfortable silence pressured Jax into filling the dead air.

"I didn't expect to keep wanting her like I do."

Chase grinned. "I knew it. You always do this. When you start a new relationship I know it will go one of two ways. If you don't really care about them, you slow play things, just using her for your personal satisfaction until someone better comes along. The ones you actually care about, you purposefully consume 24x7 until you either find something about them you don't like or get bored. It's pissing you off that you can't find anything wrong with her because she's perfect for us."

"You make me sound like an ass."

"When it comes to relationships you are an ass."

"Fuck you."

"Yes please." Chase grinned his charismatic smile that melted girl's hearts. Jaxson had to admit he wasn't immune to that smile himself. Playing sexually with Chase had started as experimentation—a rebellion against his parent's conservative mandates. Adding Emma to the mix had changed their dynamic. Jaxson could no longer pretend he didn't have real feelings towards the naked man lounging next to him any more than he could pretend to not care about Emma.

Their banter was interrupted by Emma's cell phone ringing across the room on her desk. She must have left in a hurry to forget it. Chase sprinted out of bed to grab the phone. He looked up mischievously at Jaxson after he'd read the incoming call information.

"It's her dad calling."

Jax stated the obvious. "She's avoiding him. He called twice yesterday."

"I don't know about you, but I hate that she insists on keeping us a secret." Chase looked hurt.

"I think it's refreshing, honestly. I'd rather have that than what we normally have which is people constantly using us to get attention or show off that they know a celebrity."

"I guess. Still, we're never going to get her to say yes to coming on the road with us if she won't even tell her family about us."

Jaxson knew Chase was right. Before he had time to consider the implications, the phone started ringing again. Another call from her father.

He shouldn't. It was wrong. He did it anyway.

"Hello."

There was a long hesitation at the other end of the line. "Oh, I'm sorry. I must have the wrong number. Sorry to disturb you."

"Wait... You have the right number, Mr. Fischer."

Surprise at the other end. "How do you know who I am?"

"Because I'm answering Emma's phone and she has you programmed in as 'Daddy.'"

"And why, may I ask, do you have Emma's cell phone?"

Jaxson knew he had to tread lightly here. "Emma left for class and forgot to take her phone."

"So... you are at her house? Is this Ryan?"

"No."

"Danielle's boyfriend?" He was on a fishing expedition and Jaxson was about to help him fill in the gaps.

"No, sir. I'm Emma's boyfriend." Jax felt slimy the second the words left his mouth. This was Emma's story to tell, not his. The picture of Emma losing her shit and kicking him out flashed before him just before Chase's words came back that he always does something to sabotage a relationship when he let himself start caring about someone.

Was that what he was doing? Purposefully tanking the relationship before it really got off the ground?

Only then did Jaxson realize that he had rendered Mr. Fischer speechless. He prompted the elder, "Hello? Are you still there?"

"Yes. I'm here. I'm just trying to understand why it is I'm hearing about this from you instead of my daughter."

"I'm afraid I can't answer that question, sir." Jaxson made every effort to keep his tone respectful.

"What did you say your name is again?" He was prompted.

"I didn't"

Her father sighed in exasperation. "I see. And just how long have you been seeing my little girl?"

"I met her in Europe when she was studying abroad." It was the truth. Her father didn't need to know it had literally been in her final hours there.

"Interesting. Still waiting on your name, young man."

Rarely did Jaxson feel dressed down, yet Mr. Fischer made him feel just that. "My name is Jaxson Davidson."

"Well Jaxson, I'd like you to give Emma a message to please call me the minute she gets home from her classes. We haven't seen her in several weeks. She was supposed to be coming home this weekend. Perhaps you could come with her and we could meet."

Ah. Emma the little secret keeper. "I'm not sure. We hadn't discussed it yet."

"Well Jaxson, I will be expecting you. If you are close enough to my baby girl to follow her half way across the globe, then you seem to be someone important enough for me to meet. Wouldn't you agree?"

Jaxson had opened this particular can of worms. It would be easy enough to back-pedal and say they were just friends, but the words wouldn't come. Instead he pushed forward. "I would agree, sir. In fact, another good friend of Emma's is visiting as well and if it wouldn't be too much trouble, I'd like you to meet our friend Chase as well."

"That would be fine. Perhaps you two can share your stories from Europe with us. Emma came home a changed young woman and yet she's shared very few details of her time overseas. I look forward to hearing all of the details of your time with my little girl."

He was pretty damn sure her father wouldn't be looking so forward to the stories if he knew they all entailed his daughter naked and doing the down-and-dirty with not one but two men at the same time.

"Yes, sir. I look forward to that as well."

"Very well. I'll expect to see you this weekend. Don't forget. Make sure Emma gives me a call."

The call dropped.

"You know she's gonna kick your ass for this, right?"

Jaxson did know. "Yeah, probably. Too late now."

"Well, I'm starving. Let's go down to the kitchen to grab some lunch. We should eat something just in case she decides to kick us to the curb. At least we won't be hungry."

"She won't kick us to the curb." Jaxson wished his voice didn't sound so damn unsure.

CHAPTER 12

*T*he kitchen was full when the men made it there twenty minutes later. Eating lunch with Emma's roommates was turning into a surprisingly fun daily routine. The motley crew was pretty good-natured about having two supermodels hanging out in their attic.

Emma's four unlikely roommates sat around the large kitchen table today eating big bowls of breakfast cereal for lunch. Ryan and Courtney, the only couple to live in the house, looked like they'd just finished their own marathon sex session. Danielle, the brainiac pre-law student, blushed as was normal when the men sat down at the table next to her. She then returned her attention to her computer. Very gay Richard rounded out the group. It didn't take a brain surgeon to figure out that of the group, Richard was the one most jealous of Emma. Jaxson and Chase had agreed they needed to be careful about sending the impressionable young man any wrong messages about their availability.

"Good morning," Jaxson greeted them a bit too cheerily.

"Good afternoon." Courtney teased.

Chase dished it back. "Hey, we had a late night," he said reaching to pour a cup of bad coffee.

Ryan answered him with a grin. "Yeah, we heard. I have to protest. You sex-gods are giving all men a bad name. It's inhuman how long you can go at it. You're setting very unrealistic goals for us mere mortals."

"Yeah, well there are two of us so that kinda helps." Chase teased back.

It was Courtney who probed deeper. "So how exactly does that work? I mean..."

Ryan cut her off. "I thought we discussed this, Court. It is none of your damn business how it works. Butt out."

Richard piped in. "Yeah, well I wouldn't mind hearing more about it myself."

Ryan shot his roommate a look that shut him up. Jaxson poured his cereal and milk while answering. "I'm not exactly sure what you all are fishing to know. I'd have thought you'd gotten your lesson on the birds and the bees a few years ago." He tried to make light of their teasing, unwilling to disclose personal information Emma would prefer to keep private.

He was saved from expounding by a very tired looking Emma coming through the back door into the kitchen. She dropped her too-heavy backpack to the floor with a thud before collapsing into the only empty chair with a sigh.

Not only had she not greeted them, but she wasn't even making eye contact with him.

Something was wrong.

Jaxson pushed his chair back from the table and patted his lap. "Come here, sweetheart. You look like you need a hug."

Tears sprang to her eyes as she continued to look down at her wringing hands in her lap.

Something was very wrong.

"Emma." When she glanced up briefly, he saw the confusion in her eyes. She needed his help. "My lap. Now." It was an order and it worked.

She moved slowly, but she moved. The second he wrapped his

arms around her, she dissolved into a sobbing mess, crying on his shoulder. He caught Chase's confused expression. The table went silent, waiting for Emma to stop crying. The sound of her sniffling permeated the otherwise quiet space as she slowly calmed.

Jax reached for a paper napkin on the table from the previous night's take-out Chinese. He held it up to Emma's nose. "Blow for me, baby." He used the edge of the napkin to dry the smearing mascara before pressing her for answers. "Now, who the hell upset you? I need names. Chase and I will kick their ass."

That at least got a wane smile from their curvy grad student. It didn't last long. "I don't think kicking the head of the department's ass is a good idea."

"What did he do?" Chase prodded her this time.

He noticed a flash of guilt just before she glanced away. He scooped up a spoonful of Frosted Flakes and held it to her mouth to feed her. Only after she'd eaten three bites did he continue.

"Chase asked a question, Emma. What did your professor do?" It was his Dom voice. He knew the entire house of roommates was watching the D/s dynamics of his relationship with Emma play out with fascination.

"He sat in on the class I taught today."

"And..."

"And, I wasn't as prepared as I should have been."

"And..."

"And, nothing. That's all."

He watched her closely. "Don't lie to me. What are you not telling me?"

Her eyes widened and he knew he'd been right. She had held something back.

"He has pictures."

"Of?"

"Us." It was a whisper under her breath.

"Okay. So?"

"So... there are security cameras... in places... I didn't know..."
She was blushing beet red.

Her eyes glanced around the room at her roommates before returning to his. She was panicked which meant her professor had photos of them having sex in her office.

"I see. And what does he plan on doing with said pictures?"

Her tears were back, accompanied by a healthy dose of regret. "He knows who you are."

That wasn't an answer to the question he'd asked, but it gave him a good idea of how the rest of the conversation had gone. It dawned on him he should be concerned about the photos going public, but in that moment he was more worried about what it would mean for Emma and her TA job.

"Did he fire you or threaten to go public?"

"Not exactly."

His patience with the game of fifty questions was growing thin. "Emma, just spit it out. What did he say?"

"He said he was disappointed in me. That he'd vouched for me when I was chosen as his TA and that if he'd known about my corrupt moral fiber he'd have never chosen me."

"What a prick."

"That's not all. He wrote me up for unprofessional behavior and put me on probation."

Chase had moved his chair closer and was rubbing her back to keep her calm. He piped in. "Well that doesn't sound so bad."

Emma's eyes filled with tears again. "Not so bad? Are you kidding me? I've never so much as gotten a C on a test, let alone been put on probation. It will go in my official record."

Jaxson had to hide his smile. In the wide spectrum of things, this wasn't that big of a deal, but then it hit him. If she was this upset over being chastised in private for something so insignificant, how was she going to handle the likely public outcry if they went public with their ménage relationship?

It was in that moment that Jaxson knew he had every intention of continuing their relationship even after their summer vacation was over. One way or another, he wanted Emma in his life. The tension that had started to build again the day before suddenly slipped away, leaving him at peace with the knowledge that he was, in fact, in a relationship with Emma and Chase. Not a fuck-fest. Not a down-low interlude. No. They were in a real relationship. That could mean only one thing.

"I'll go talk to him. What is his name?"

"Oh God, no. Not that. That would make it worse."

"Trust me. I've got this."

"That's not even all. I lost my damn phone today, too. I've retraced my steps and can't find it. I hope no one breaks into it because I have a lot of..." She paused, glancing around with panic at her roommates before continuing a bit more subdued, "...photos I wouldn't want to get into the wrong hands."

Jaxson had taken most of them and agreed the X-rated photos of the three in all kinds of kinky positions needed to stay private.

Chase jumped in a bit too cheerily. "You didn't lose it. You left it upstairs in the bedroom." Had he stopped there, all would have been fine. He didn't stop. "Your dad called."

Jaxson shot him a look that could kill weaker men.

"You didn't answer it, did you?" She prompted Chase with alarm.

"Oh no. I didn't." Jax felt her body relax at the news Chase hadn't talk to her father. It was short lived. "But Jaxson did."

She twisted around in his arms, a shocked look on her face. "You didn't," she accused.

"I did." He boasted authoritatively as if he'd had every right to answer her phone. Meanwhile, the frosted flakes churned in his stomach, knowing he'd been a prick to put the woman he cared about in this position with her family.

"And?" He saw anger flashing in her eyes, which had his defenses flaring.

"He thinks you're coming home for a visit. He wants to meet

us." He felt slimy, but he went on offense. "Can you tell me why this is the first Chase and I are hearing about you leaving for the weekend?"

She hedged. "Um... I forgot."

"Really? Is that the story you're gonna stick with?"

Guilt rolled off her in waves. "It's just that... well... fuck."

"Precisely. Fuck is right."

Courtney and Ryan were grinning as their roommate squirmed in Jaxson's arms, trying to escape his lap. He held her firm. "I think we should take this discussion upstairs, don't you young lady?" Despite his guilt for answering her phone, Emma's innocent wide eyes looking at him submissively had his cock filling under her wiggling ass. A curvy ass he had a sudden urge to see turn as pink as her blushing cheeks.

Richard piped in, almost breathless with excitement. "No need. I mean we can hear everything down here anyway in this old house."

Jaxson knew he was being a dick but he couldn't resist. He felt up her bottom through her jeans and she writhed in his arms, trying to scramble away. He swatted her ass several times in quick succession and she stopped her struggles. He scooped her into his arms and took off for the back stairs, throwing his reply over his shoulder.

"Oh stay tuned, Richard. If you thought we were loud before when we were having sex, just wait until you hear how loud our girl here is when I use my belt on this naughty bottom of hers. Come along Chase."

He heard the shocked gasp from Emma's roommates as he hustled them upstairs for some veiled privacy.

CHAPTER 13

*C*hase went ahead of them as they got to the final staircase. He opened the door, allowing Jaxson to sweep in with Emma still wriggling in his arms. He crossed to the bed and dropped her into the mess of unmade sheets and she tried to scramble away with a yelp. He caught her by the ankle, her summer sandal falling to the floor.

He pulled her body back towards him at the edge. The three of them hadn't spoke yet, but there was a shared heaviness in the silence. Gone was the carefree play of the last two weeks, replaced by an unexpected urgency as the outside world began to close in on them. Emma's family and her professor were forcing them to contemplate their future whether they wanted to or not.

Emma and Chase followed his lead, six hands moved in unison to peel off the first piece of clothing they came into contact with. Tension was still rolling off Emma and he knew exactly how to resolve it.

"Lay down in the middle of the bed, sweetheart. On your tummy."

"You aren't going to..."

"Don't worry about it. You're not in trouble. I'm gonna make you feel better."

She didn't look too sure, but she followed directions, stretching her hands submissively above her head to grasp onto the headboard rails as he'd taught her weeks before. On cue, Chase worked to secure her wrists in the waiting fur-lined restraints, ensuring their submissive would stay in place for whatever lay ahead.

"Chase, sit there at the head of the bed and massage Emma's shoulders and neck." While Chase followed directions, Jaxson massaged her lower back, dipping down to squeeze her rounded ass cheeks. She might not be a hard-core submissive, but he had spanked her enough to know it was exactly what she needed right this minute to get her mind off being put on probation.

He lifted his palm and brought it down sharply across her bare right globe. A surprised chirp filled the room followed by a soft moan he took as a sign to continue. The second and third slap came quickly, followed by a louder groan.

He looked at Chase. He saw understanding in his friend's eyes. Chase pressed Emma's shoulders down to keep her stationary as Jaxson started the spanking in earnest. Several dozen swats in, Jaxson stopped only long enough to push Emma's legs farther apart, angling her feet towards the corners of the bed and lifting her to her knees, exposing her wet pussy for his inspection.

Emma's whimpers turned to a soft cry. He was expecting it when she tried to pull free. She always panicked just before she finally turned herself over to the pain. That release was where he was driving her to today. She needed it. When she started jerking on her cuffs in hopes of reaching back to block her spanking, Chase stroked her hair and leaned in to whisper into her ear, telling her what a good girl she was and how proud he was of her.

His gentle words broke her emotional dam. Chase helped her lift her upper body from the bed just enough to slip under her, leaning his back against the headboard between her locked wrists so she was resting her upper body in his embrace. Jax gave her a moment of respite as Chase stroked her long brunette hair slowly... reverently.

The men's eyes met behind their submissive's back and the longing he saw etched on Chase's face surprised Jax. While he himself still fought to hold Chase and Emma at arm's length, it was clear Chase had torn down his own emotional wall, laying his raw passion on the line.

Jaxson felt an uncharacteristic moment of jealousy as he watched his lovers comfort each other with loving caresses and murmurs that sounded like promises of love. Warmth spread through Jaxson's chest when Chase turned that look of love on him. His lover shone his sunshine persona on Jaxson and in that moment, he felt closer to Chase and Emma than he had with any other human beings in his life. The emotional intimacy should have alarmed him, but all he could honestly admit to was feeling relief.

Relief at finally finding home. Relief that he wouldn't have to be alone anymore. Relief that he could officially stop the bullshit of pretending to be happy about being an aloof asshole. Relief at realizing he had not one but two amazing people who wanted him to lead them to the next level of their complicated relationship.

He felt the need to mark the moment—to own his remarkable decision like a badge— to assert his rightful position in their unique trio. His eyes locked with Chase's normally jovial gaze, communicating the loving feelings he wasn't able to verbalize yet.

His hands fell to the belt of his jeans. With purpose he unbuckled the large silver clasp, slowly pulling the belt out of its loops. The swoosh of leather nipping the air as it flicked free brought a shiver to their naked submissive. Jaxson's intention to deliver lines of heat to the curvy woman's bottom would most likely seem barbaric to an unwelcome voyeur to their erotic scene, but the three occupants of the attic understood the pain helped make the pleasure more intense. It produced a cocktail of emotions they had all become addicted to.

Chase wiggled to take his own T-Shirt off and unbuckled his jeans, pushing them down just enough to expose his hardening cock.

"Take Chase in your mouth, Emma." Jaxson ordered.

She lunged down, her arms stretching out to reach. Only once her mouth and throat were full of man-meat did Jaxson apply the two-inch worn leather to stripe across the middle of her ass. Emma and Chase moaned in unison, the vibrations of her moan against his cock in her mouth, bringing him enhanced pleasure.

Jaxson delivered another stroke, aiming a bit lower and eliciting a louder reaction. Two more stripes followed in quick succession with Emma's ass rocking back and forth from front to back as if she were trying to get away from the sting.

He wasn't striking her hard. Would she still feel it later when she sat down for dinner? Certainly. Would it be painful or merely a warm tingling glow that brought her pleasure? He was going for the latter. His fingers slipped between her legs to stroke the wetness pooling there, confirming he was giving her exactly what she needed.

Chase had closed his eyes, enjoying the feeling of Emma taking him in her mouth so Jaxson continued on, moving the belt lower across her tender sit-spot and down to her pale thighs. After a particularly hard connection, Jaxson noticed her shaved pussy lips contracting as if trying to squeeze an imaginary cock. It was time to feed her desire.

The belt hit the hardwood floor as he unzipped his jeans and dropped them to the ground. He was on the bed, on his knees behind her in seconds. She was devouring Chase's cock, bobbing up and down as she gagged herself again and again. Jaxson knew the signs and warned Chase, "Don't come. Not until we are all ready. We go together."

Agony and bliss filled the handsome model's face in equal

measure as Emma continued to face-fuck herself on his tool. She seemed consumed with desire to the point of not realizing what was about to happen to her body. Jaxson pinned Chase with a stare as his cock thrust forward to bury himself in Emma's folds. All three of the lovers cried out with satisfaction as their bodies fit together like a puzzle.

He set a fast pace, urged on by the growing emotional connection he felt to the two people linked to him intimately. In an odd moment of clarity, Jax acknowledged his goal for his month off had changed. He was no longer trying to work Emma out of his system. He was no longer just playing with Chase to experiment or even piss off his father.

This was real. This was right. As he roared his climax, he buried himself as deep as her body would allow. Emma squeezed his tool like a vise as her own orgasm rocked her body. Jaxson opened his eyes just in time to watch Chase tip into his own pleasure, filling Emma's mouth with warm jizz.

Jaxson and Emma toppled over to the bed, suddenly exhausted. Chase unbuckled her wrists before settling himself next to them. The three lovers lay recovering, body parts tangled, skin damp from their exertion. The quiet moment was perfect so Emma's outburst surprised him.

"Don't think that amazing tryst made me forget how mad I am at you for answering my phone. I can't fucking believe you told my father we were dating."

"Hey, watch it little girl. That didn't sound very respectful." Jaxson squeezed the heavy breast he had been caressing before her outburst as added warning.

He didn't like it when she pushed herself away from him, disengaging enough to crawl over Chase and out of the bed. She stood looking down at him, her arms crossed, the most adorable defiance on her sex-flushed face. Under normal circumstances, he would enjoy spanking her into submission, but there was nothing normal about any of the heavy shit going on in their lives right now.

She only made it worse when she spoke, "I'll respect you when you have earned it. That was really shitty, Jax."

"Oh really, Em. It's so awesome of you to hide us from your parents. To lie about going home this weekend because you're too ashamed to be seen with us in public."

She shouted her reply. "Oh really, Jaxson. Well, what's your excuse for refusing to answer Roberta's calls? Is it so you can avoid telling her about why you're here in Wisconsin? I know it's because you're too embarrassed to admit you're playing with a curvy co-ed for a few weeks."

Jaxson was on his feet in a flash, gripping her biceps and shaking her as if to put some sense into her. "Listen, I know you're mad at me, but don't you dare try to compare my silence to yours. I'm trying to protect you from the bullshit that comes with being on her radar. I've never wanted to hide us."

Chase was on his feet, trying to wedge himself between them, the consummate peacekeeper. "Alright, everyone calm down. You are both right to be upset."

Jax and Emma both shot him daggers, but Chase continued on fearlessly. "Oh, stop. Emma, don't look so innocent. We would have gladly taken out a full-page ad to announce we were in town if you wanted us to. You are the one who has insisted on keeping our identity here secret. I don't give a shit about anyone else, but I'm hurt too that you don't trust us enough to tell your parents about how important we are to you."

For the first time in the argument she looked contrite and Jaxson was starting to feel vindicated until Chase turned his anger on his direction.

"And you, Jax, never should have answered her phone. That was an invasion of privacy. I'm as hurt as you are that she doesn't want to tell them about us, not because it hurts my ego, but I just know that if she can't tell them, then she'll never be brave enough to leave with us when it's time to go and that breaks my heart."

His words hit home. As always, Chase had his sexy finger on the emotional temperature of the moment.

Emma broke the uncomfortable silence with a whispered confession. "I'm sorry, but I just didn't want to tell them because I didn't want them feeling sorry for me after you guys leave me. It's going to be hard enough to move on with my roommates knowing and asking about you. And I didn't want our final weeks together to be full of sadness and stress."

The weight of Emma's looming sadness hit Jaxson in the gut. He hated the thought of hurting her. The sound of Roberta's ringtone filled the air. His eyes met Chase's. He could feel the pressure closing in on him. He was supposed to have all of the answers, yet everything and everyone important to him felt out of control. Rather than reaching for his phone, he bent to pull on a rumpled pair of jogging shorts and a University of Wisconsin T-shirt.

He was half way to the door when he let them know, "I'm going for a run." He had just put a ball cap and sunglasses on when he heard Emma's angry "What a hypocrite."

Jaxson dashed out of the room, leaving his still ringing cell phone behind. He only wished he could leave the pressing guilt of hurting the only people he cared about behind as easily.

* * *

THREE MILES LATER, Jaxson found himself standing in front of the College of Business building on campus. He was sweaty and out of breath after his long run. He wanted to be angry with Emma and Chase, but all he'd been able to sort out as he pressed his body hard was that he felt out of control and he hated it.

It had been years since he'd felt this out of control. It had been back when he was an undergrad at NYU when his father was running for US Senator that things had come to a head. It had been Chase even then who had shown him that he didn't have to play the role of victim when his father had tried to capitalize on Jaxson's growing fame as a top model. He had taken control then, and by God, he would get things back under control now.

And his first stop was to have a discussion with the head of Emma's department. No one would get away with hurting her on his watch.

The building directory in the lobby gave him the location of Professor Harold Kanowski, Dean of the College of Business. Jaxson stopped in a men's room he passed just long enough to splash some cold water on his face and pat down the sweat he'd worked up while running.

It was late in the afternoon and Jax was relieved there were only a few students in the building between summer classes. He arrived at the closed door of the Dean's office, and knocked loudly. At first he thought the office must be empty, but then he heard a shuffling inside just before a gruff shout told him to go away. Jaxson's sixth sense told him to press his luck so he pounded on the door even louder the second time.

The professor's angry voice shouted, "I'm busy. Come back during office hours."

He was hoping he wouldn't regret it when he tested the door-knob, surprised to find the door unlocked. Jaxson took a deep breath and pushed the entry open.

The overhead lights in the office were off, but the hot after-noon sun shining through the second story blinds was more than bright enough for Jaxson to see the bobbing head in the over-weight professor's lap behind the desk. The older man was distracted enough by the mouth slurping as it sucked his cock that he hadn't heard Jaxson open the door. Today was Jaxson's lucky day, although he suspected the professor's was about to go to shit.

"Well what have we here?" He cleared his throat loudly. He suspected he had scared the person on their knees between the professor's legs because the older man cried out in pain as if he'd been nicked by a tooth.

"Jesus Christ! I told you to come back..." His voice trailed off as his eyes met Jaxson's. Recognition registered just before he quickly pushed his rolling chair back, distancing himself from the hidden body behind his desk. The teacher fumbled to tuck his deflating cock back into his khakis.

Jaxson couldn't resist taunting him. "My apologies, professor. It seems I've interrupted something."

It wasn't until the person under the desk crawled out on their hands and knees and pushed to stand that Jaxson understood exactly what he'd disrupted.

"Well, well, well. This is a surprise, indeed. I wonder what Mrs. Kanowski would say about this development. Hello, young man." Jaxson grinned at the too-thin pimple-faced kid who had to be barely of age while the professor's face turned red with rage.

"Get the hell out of here, Tommy."

"But professor, you're still gonna change my grade, right? I mean you said only if I swallowed, but it's not my fault he came in here too soon."

"GET. THE. FUCK. OUT. OF. HERE!"

Jaxson had to step aside to let the now running student rush out the door, a look of sheer terror on his face. He closed the door quietly, before turning to square off with the asshole who had blackmailed his Emma. The elder stared back at him, defiance warring with fear.

"I wonder if there are any cameras in this office?" Jaxson taunted before continuing. "Boy, the story they could tell if there were." The professor remained stoic, letting Jaxson do all of the talking. "No, I'm guessing there aren't any camera's in here, are there, professor? You'd never want to risk pictures getting back to your wife."

"Don't try to blackmail me, young man."

"Oh, you mean like you did Emma just a few hours ago?"

"Her behavior was unacceptable. Emma is a student teacher here."

"Exactly, so a single woman having consensual sex with two non-students is no big deal. You, on the other hand, are a married professor. A person in power, having sex with a young student in exchange for changing grades. I'm not sure, but I think that is a no-no at most universities."

"You have no proof. As you said, there are no cameras in here."

Jaxson laughed, "And how hard do you think it would be for me to find other students who would come forward to out the hard-ass professor who blackmailed them into blowjobs for better grades?"

The man behind the desk looked like he had swallowed something sour. Almost a full minute of silence passed before he countered, "What do you want?"

Jaxson was ready. "I want you to apologize to Emma and I want you to remove any trace of her probation from her record."

"It's too late. I already filed the paperwork."

"Then you have a problem, don't you?"

Professor Kanowski's face turned victorious. "I'll go public with the video. I'm pretty sure the local news station would love to get footage of two celebrity men fucking a young woman and each other."

Jaxson's voice filled with venom. "Get your story straight, asshole. What Emma, Chase and I do is a lot more than fucking."

The professor laughed victoriously, not understanding Jaxson's point. "Well it sure looked like fucking to me. I admit, seeing Emma's tits as you plowed her got me all hot and bothered. I'm sure once it hits the Internet, the world will enjoy jacking off to it almost as much as I did."

Jaxson was around the desk in a flash, pulling the professor to his feet before slamming him against the wall of bookshelves. Several books from the upper shelves fell on the men from the velocity of the crash.

"Listen up, you asshole. I'm not going to let you hurt my Emma."

"Your Emma? Christ, you sound like you actually care about her."

"Damn right I care."

"Oh come on. The door is closed. There is no camera. It's just you and me so you don't have to keep up the lie."

The fact that this man found it impossible that a man like Jaxson could be in love with Emma frankly pissed him off. Would this be everyone's reaction when they went public?

It was then that he understood why Emma wasn't answering her parent's phone calls. Why he was avoiding Roberta and why he dreaded seeing his own father.

Why did the world have to be so fucking judgmental? Well fuck the world. The last few weeks of hiding at Emma's had been wonderful, but vacation was over. It was time to go public. For the first time all day he felt back in control.

His first order of business was to set things right with the jack-off in front of him. "You're a real prick, you know that? I'm gonna make this easy for you. You have exactly twenty-four hours to apologize to Emma and to squash the probation or I go to the press. As you pointed out, I'm a celebrity. When we go public, the papers are going to eat up my relationship with Emma and Chase. And when I have the spotlight, don't think the same reporters won't be interested in listening when I tell them about the Dean of Business who is blackmailing students into sex for grades."

"You wouldn't."

"Try me."

Jaxson was almost out the door when the man's taunt made it to him. "You're some piece of work. You have Emma believing you wanted her to leave school to go on the road with you. If that were true, you should be happy she might get kicked out of school. Then she'd be free to go away with you. This is probably your way of getting rid of her when you're done with your fun."

Jaxson stopped in his tracks, not bothering to turn around to face the jerk who'd hurt Emma. "You don't know shit about me. I want Emma to come away with Chase and me, but she needs to do it because she chooses to. Not because she has no other choice. Twenty-four hours."

Jaxson closed the door behind him, leaving the professor to contemplate his next move.

CHAPTER 14

*T*he attic was oppressively hot the next morning when
Jaxson stirred awake. As always, they had slept curled
up together after making love into the night. He was thinking
about how nice it would be to get back to their king-sized beds on
the road when it struck him that there might be only two of them
in that bed after they left. They hadn't talked about Emma leaving
with them again the night before after he'd returned from his run.
Instead they had each tried to win an academy award for their
ability to hide from the eight-hundred pound gorilla hanging
around their necks like a noose.

Time was ticking down and they all knew it.

Emma was curled up in front of him with Chase spooning her
from behind. He hadn't opened his eyes yet, but he didn't need to
to know his lovers were awake too. The heavy blanket of their
unknown future weighed on Jaxson. It was Friday morning. Only
one day to sort out if the men would be accompanying Emma to
visit her family over the weekend. As much as he'd like to, this is
one area where he knew he couldn't dominate Emma's decision.

The first sound to fill the room was another cell phone.

"We should all turn our damn phones off." Chase's uncharacteristic grouse surprised Jaxson.

"At least it's not my dad again," Emma sighed, leaning up and over Jaxson to grab her phone from the nightstand. "Oh my God. It's my professor. He's kicking me out. I just know it."

Jaxson hadn't told them about his detour to visit with the slimy professor the day before and he wanted to keep it that way. "Just answer it and see what he has to say."

She answered tentatively, "Hello?"

Emma listened, her breath becoming shorter as time passed. She tried to interrupt the call several times, but wasn't successful until she finally asked, "But what about the video? You're going to keep that private?"

Jaxson could see the worry lines receding from her forehead as tears came to her eyes. It appeared the good professor had taken his threats seriously.

Emma ended the call, a huge grin on her face. "Wow. He called to tell me he had second thoughts and has rescinded my probation. He even apologized for how he treated me. Can you believe that?"

Emma was distracted by the phone call, but Jaxson felt Chase's stare from the other side of the bed. When their eyes met, Chase's grin told him at least one of his lovers had figured out why the asshole had had a change of heart.

The silent air kiss Chase playfully sent his way made Jaxson's heart contract with emotion. Chase knew him so well. He was so much more than his lover. He was his best friend. Whatever happened over the next few weeks as they sorted their relationship out, one thing was for sure—Jaxson needed to protect his friendship with Chase first and foremost.

Emma hadn't even settled back into bed when the next phone rang. This time it was Roberta's ring. And just like that, the heavy blanket was dousing them. Worry filled Chase's gaze again. Jaxson needed to deal with this. Delaying the inevitable wasn't helping any of them any more.

He reached for the phone and hit ANSWER just in the nick of time. "Hey, Roberta."

"God dammit, Jaxson. What the fuck is going on? I jumped through hoops to get you a few weeks off and how do you repay me? You drop off the fucking face of the earth, refusing to take my calls. You'd better have some damn good excuse, buddy. I've been lying my ass off to keep you two from losing the most lucrative contract I've ever gotten for you, so don't you fucking dare hang up on me."

Jaxson sighed, "We've missed you too, Roberta."

"Don't try to charm your way out of this, buddy. I'm pissed. I don't deserve this shit. You're giving me grey hair. I hate grey hair!"

Jaxson chuckled at her melodramatic rant. It was so Roberta. She was an awesome agent and she was right about one thing. She didn't deserve to be lied to any more.

"Okay, well I'll start by saying I'm sorry. How about that?"

There was a pause at the other end of the phone. "Who the hell is this and how did you get Jaxson's phone?"

"Ha, ha. Very funny. What exactly is it you need from us? We still have two more weeks off."

"Well that's just it. You only have ten more days, not two weeks."

"No. I distinctly remember us committing to being back on the first."

"Yes, well that was before I nabbed you the Abercrombie fall promotion. They had already started shooting and hated the first review enough they are changing directions completely. They are willing to sign a full years contract just to get you two specifically. When I couldn't reach you, I was able to buy you another week, but you absolutely must be in London by next weekend."

He felt Emma and Chase staring at his back as he stared out

the only window to look down on the driveway. His heart was racing as he thought through their options. He expected to feel trapped, but a welcome calmness settled instead. He knew his way forward.

He spun to face his lovers before answering his agent and manager. "Alright, we'll meet you in London, but not before that Monday. That will be four days earlier than I promised. That has to be good enough."

He could hear her cussing under her breath before answering. He could see the tears welling in Emma's eyes as Roberta answered in his ear. "You can be a real pain in my ass, you know that Jax? It's a damn good thing you and Chase make me a lot of money. I'm going to need it to recover later. I assume Chase is still with you, right? You'll tell him?"

"Yep. We'll see you in London on Tuesday, the twenty-eighth."

"No. On Monday, the twenty-seventh."

"Bye Roberta." He ended the call before she could pressure him more.

Not a word had been spoken when his phone rang again. "Dammit Roberta, We're coming back four days early. That has to be good enough."

"Hello Jaxson."

Fuck. He should have looked at his phone to see who it was.

"Father. I guess it's too late to hang up and pretend I missed your call."

"I've missed you too, son."

He was annoyed by his father's smug banter. "So what do you need today, Senator?"

"Can't I just call my son to see how he's doing? You haven't been home in over a year. Surely they let you have a vacation at some point."

He shouldn't get joy out of hurting his father, but he did. "As a matter a fact, I've been on vacation for several weeks now."

The silence on the line assured Jaxson his barb had hit home.

"Like I said, what do you need?"

Before his father answered, Jaxson heard a muffled argument at the other end of the line. The sound of his father cussing out the poor man in the process of shining his shoes for missing a spot reminded Jaxson of what a pretentious asshole his old man was.

His father returned to the call, unaware of Jaxson's growing anger. "I thought you'd like to know that I will be announcing my candidacy for President at a gala in DC next Saturday."

So the reports on the news had been right. Jaxson wasn't surprised. The only thing his father had ever cared about was power and money. He had proven that when the senator had sold his own mother's ancestral homestead for several million to a development group against her wishes. The cherry on the top had been his shoving the brokenhearted woman into a retirement home, never visiting her and leaving her to die an early death alone. Jaxson had sworn as he had stood at his grandmother's grave at the age of fifteen that he would be sure to treat his father with the exact same disregard he had shown his own mother.

"President, you say. I didn't know you wanted to be president of the PTA. I thought you had to still have a kid in school to be elected to the board of parents."

"I see you still haven't outgrown your angry phase, son."

"Sorry *Dad*, but I'm afraid this isn't just a phase. Thanks for the info. Tell Mom I say hi. Oh yeah, I forgot. You don't speak to her either unless it's in front of the cameras."

"How would you know? You're never here."

"Touché. Well..."

"Wait. Jaxson?" Here it comes. He always wanted something. "My campaign manager says it's critical that you be there on stage with your mother and me when we make the announcement."

Jaxson sighed, "Of course it is. Have to keep up the image of the All-American family and all, right? Maybe we can bake cookies afterwards and play a board game."

"You don't have to be such an ass about this, you know."

"See, that's where I think you're wrong. I'm assuming you'd look for my endorsement of your campaign?"

"Is that a rhetorical question?"

"Still voting against anything that might help minorities? How about your stance on immigration? Let me guess, still preaching that the LGBT community deserves to burn in hell?"

"Enough. You only support those causes to piss me off."

"I hate to burst your bubble, Dad, but I actually believe you and your cronies are wrong on almost every topic. It's life-long politicians like you that are driving our country into the ground."

"What do you know about it, Jaxson? You spend your time gallivanting around the world on yachts getting your picture taken for the tabloids and drinking champagne. Save me the lecture." His father took a deep breath, apparently remembering he had called to ask for a favor and realizing screaming at Jax may not be the best way to manipulate him into compliance. He finished with a quiet, "You owe me."

The plan came to him in a flash. "For the record, I don't owe you shit, Dad, but I don't want to fight with you anymore. I'll come and smile for the cameras. The world can have their photos of the perfect First Family, but then I'm out of there. Don't ask me to go on the road for you or any shit like that."

He heard the surprise in the elder man's voice. "Really? You'll come? I can have them advertise it?"

"Yeah, I'll give you one night."

"Thank you, Jaxson."

"Just have Bonnie send me the details." He hung up without saying good-bye.

Chase was in his face within seconds. "What the fuck was that, Jaxson? You didn't even ask me and now you have us going back early? And you swore you'd never help your father get elected to dog catcher, let alone lend him your support for the presidency."

Emma had tears falling down her cheeks, yesterday's mascara

smeared adorably under her eyes like a raccoon. She had no idea how refreshing that was for Jaxson. The models he was used to dating would never let him see them without their full face on. Emma was real. He wouldn't... no *couldn't*... lose her.

"Relax, Chase. I'm not going." He made sure they were listening carefully before continuing. "*We're* going. We can't stay holed up in the attic forever and we'll make a stop in DC on the way to London."

He closed the distance to Emma, holding her close and looking down into her glistening eyes. Chase stepped up to hold her from behind, sandwiching her between them.

"Come with us, Emma. Please." He hated the vulnerability he heard in his voice.

The tears were overflowing down her cheeks. He reached out to swish them away with the pad of his thumb, caressing her cheek softly as if he were afraid to frighten her away.

"But what will happen when you guys get tired of me? When you realize I'm the third wheel you don't need anymore? I mean, surely you're going to meet some gorgeous, famous A-listers and want to settle down. Threesome's like ours don't make it in the light of day.

Chase was chuckling, rubbing against her suggestively. "Honey, we are consenting adults and we can have any kind of relationship we damn-well want. And for the record, Jaxson was raised with A-listers. He's been surrounded by the rich and famous his whole life. Why do you think he's with us?"

Chase's gaze locked on Jaxson before he continued seriously. "It's what I love about him the most. He will always be loyal to those who love him, not to those with the biggest bank accounts, fame or power."

The word love hung in the air between them. He had known Chase loved him as his best friend, but today the word felt different. More important. *Real.*

"Chase... I..."

111

The blond man's grin defused the heaviness of the moment. "It's okay, baby. I know you aren't ready to say it yet, but I am. I love you Jaxson Davidson just like I love Emma. You two may still be dicking around trying to fight it, but I'm on record for saying it first. I don't want this to end. Ever. I want to spend the rest of my life with you both. Just like this. Having freaking hot sex. Traveling the world. Growing old together. Raising kids together. The works. And I'd really appreciate it if you would both get your heads out of your asses and get with the program here."

Jaxson couldn't tear his eyes away from Chase, even when he heard Emma sobbing between them. She wiggled herself around in his arms to turn and tackle Chase, pelting him with kisses on his bare chest and neck as the men held their visual connection.

Jaxson's heart was racing. They were in uncharted territory and yet it felt good. "That was a pretty important speech you gave there. You thinking of running for office one day, like my dad?"

The smile that lit up Chase's handsome face gutted him. "Just for the PTA."

Jaxson couldn't wait another second. He rushed forward, crushing Emma between them as he crashed his mouth to Chase's in a searing kiss. The men's tongues dueled, igniting the fire that was always just below the surface when the three of them were together. The intensity of their passion was like a drug for them all, taking them flying high.

Only the sound of yet another cell phone ringing could distract them. The men caught their breath as they leaned in, their foreheads touching intimately as Emma wiggled from between them. They snapped together like magnets, pressing close so their aroused cocks rubbed against each other. Jaxson felt the wetness of Chase's pre-cum smearing against his groin, flaming his own desire.

The sound of Emma talking to her parents doused the fire just a bit. "Yes, Daddy. Actually, I'm glad. I need to talk to you and Mom too. Okay. Bye."

Emma turned back towards them and he could see she was fighting the return of her panic. "They're almost here. They want to take me to lunch. They're worried about me."

She crossed to her dresser and began taking out a bra and panties before reaching into her armoire for a summer dress. "I'm gonna take a quick shower."

Chase reassured her. "Yeah, you go first. It takes you longer to dry your hair. Jax and I can be ready to go in just a few minutes after our shower."

Jax could see her struggling to answer, so he answered for her. "Emma is going alone, aren't you honey?"

She looked nervous. Like she was waiting for him to get angry.

Chase *was* angry, "I thought we were past this shit. I told you I loved you, God dammit."

Emma crossed to their lover and smiled as she stroked the sexy scruff on his cheek as she answered, "And it means the world to me. It really does, Chase. But I still need to go alone, at least this first time. I owe that much to my parents. They need to hear the truth from me first. Let them get used to the idea before they meet you."

"But..."

She cut him off. "Please. Trust me. I need to do this on my own."

She didn't wait for the men to answer. She just picked up the rest of the toiletries she'd need and headed down the stairs to the shared bathroom on the second floor, leaving the men alone.

CHAPTER 15

*E*mma had been gone almost two hours when the doorbell rang. The men had been conveniently avoiding talking about the heavy things happening by battling each other in Halo 3. Chase jumped up to look out the small window.

"There's a sedan I've never seen in the driveway."

The loud clumping of heavy feet rushing up the wooden stairs to the attic could be heard over the video game. Jaxson grabbed the remote to flick off the power just as the pounding on the bedroom door started.

The men looked at each other nervously, suspecting who might be on the other side of the thankfully thick door. Jaxson moved quietly towards the door, hoping to get it locked before whoever was on the other side burst in to find the naked men.

"Jaxson Davidson and Chase Cartwright, I know you're in there. This is Emma's father. Open up."

The men's "fuck" was in unison.

It must have carried behind the door because Mr. Fischer's response was to pound louder. "My sentiments exactly. Now open this door."

Jaxson looked around the space they'd been holed up in

for the last few weeks and knew without a doubt he'd be dead within minutes if he let Emma's father inside. It was one big sex playroom. Restraints, dildos, vibrators, and punishment devices of all shapes and sizes covered most open spaces. The messed bed still bore the sticky remains of multiple orgasms.

Jaxson made it to the door just in time to hold it closed as the elder Fischer started to open it.

"Hello, Mr. Fischer. This is Jaxson. We'll be happy to talk with you. We'll meet you downstairs in five minutes."

"No, we'll talk here. Now."

Chase looked worried and started to frantically try to pick up the most racy of sex toys just in case Emma's father made it past Jaxson.

Jaxson held his ground. "No, sir. I insist. We'll talk in the kitchen."

"You listen to me, young man. I love my daughter very much and I'm coming in there this instant."

Chase froze, turning to stare at Jaxson with panicked eyes. Jaxson met his heated stare as he replied, "And I love your daughter too, and that's why I insist that you not come in here now. Trust me, sir. We are best to talk downstairs."

Despite the seriousness of the situation, Chase's victorious grin at Jaxson's declaration of love warmed him.

Emma's father cursed, "God damn it. Fine. You have five minutes."

Jaxson waited until he heard the retreating steps before letting go of the door. Chase was still grinning from ear to ear, his arms crossed across his bare chest, the jutting cock Jaxson loved so much swinging between his legs.

"What the hell are you smiling at? He's pissed!" Jaxson questioned.

If possible, Chase's grin grew. "I knew it. You love us."

Jaxson chuckled as he reached for a pair of jeans thrown over the back of the desk chair. "I said I loved Emma. I didn't say shit about you."

Chase knew him well. "Uh-huh. Right." Damned if he still stood there, staring at Jaxson. They'd been best friends for years, so it felt odd to feel uncomfortable with Chase, but he was in new territory and they both knew it.

"Shut up, will you? This is serious."

Chase took a tentative step forward, moving in Jaxson's direction slowly. "Yes, it is serious. It isn't every day the man I'm in love with admits he loves me back."

Jaxson stood frozen, waiting until his lover entered his personal space. The men closed the final inches between them, their mouths crushing together as Jaxson weaved his fingers through Chase's long hair, holding his head stationary as he plundered his mouth with a probing tongue. He felt Chase melting against his body like the submissive that he was.

Jaxson moved his left hand down to grip Chase's thickening cock, dragging a tortured moan from his lover. When Jax pulled out of the kiss, their labored breathing filled the room. "You need to put this bad boy back to sleep until later. I don't think we need him for what's coming next."

Chase's "Yes, sir," was perfect and had Jaxson's own cock filling.

It took all of their willpower to separate and dress respectably for the important meeting ahead.

Five minutes later the men stepped into the large kitchen. Emma's father stood at the window looking out on the backyard, his arms crossed defensively. He didn't turn to greet them when they entered.

Their housemate, Richard, sat at the kitchen table, eyes wide, looking as if he had a front row seat to the best show in town.

"Richard, can you please leave us alone for a few minutes? We have some private topics to discuss."

The gay man who was infatuated with his houseguests protested, "But, I want to stay."

Jaxson enlisted his best Dom voice to urge Richard's compliance. "Richard. Now. Leave."

The student's eyes widened before he uttered a quick, "Yes, sir," and scurried off.

Only once the three men were alone did Emma's dad turn. They stood off, silently sizing each other up before her dad broke the silence. "I see you're a man used to calling the shots. That explains how my little girl fell under your spell. I couldn't believe she'd be swayed by money and fame alone."

Of all of the words the man could have uttered, these were not going to get them off to a good start. "I resent that. Emma has never asked us for a thing. Nothing. Do you know how rare that is in my life?"

"That doesn't surprise me. She's young. Impressionable. A good girl."

"Yes. But don't forget intelligent. Beautiful. Honorable." He saw her father's surprise at his praise. "You did a great job of raising her, but..." Jaxson paused, weighting every word carefully. "But she's not a girl any more. She's a woman."

Apparently those were not the right words, as her father's face only got redder. "Don't talk to me about her being a woman. You've corrupted her. What exactly are your intentions with my daughter? She's talking nonsense of quitting school and following you half way around the world."

Jaxson had to fight down his joy at hearing that Emma was seriously considering going with them when they left soon. A glance sideways showed a beaming Chase, happy with the news that Emma would be going with them to London. Obviously her father's gaze followed Jaxson's as he turned to Chase too for the first time. "And what's your story? Are you some type of puppy dog following him around too? Why are you here watching Jaxson take advantage of my daughter? I'd think you'd have your own woman to corrupt."

The glow on Chase's face extinguished in a defeated rush.

Jaxson saw the pain in his lover's eyes as Chase internalized that Emma had only told her parents about her relationship with Jaxson... not Chase. Tears glistened in Chase's adorable brown eyes and Jaxson felt his pain. Without thinking of the implications, he closed the distance between them and leaned in close to whisper in Chase's ear. "You were right. I love you too."

The men's light kiss had just begun when the back door slammed open and an out of breath Emma barged in, an attractive middle-aged woman fast on her heels.

"Daddy! I can't believe you did that! We had to walk all the way from the diner." Emma's eyes scanned the room, falling on her lovers, a look of relief at finding them still alive and in one piece.

Her father filled the awkward silence by telling his wife what she'd missed. "There is something really fishy going on here. I don't want you mixed up in this, Emma."

"Dad, it's too late for that. I'm already all in."

"But you don't understand. They kissed each other!" The older man was scandalized.

Emma reached out to pat his arm, trying to calm him. "Yes, Dad. I know. That's what happens with people who are in love."

Jaxson was surprised to see relief on the elder's face. "So what are you? Just a diversion to hide their gay relationship?"

Jaxson held his breath, waiting to see how Emma would respond and relieved when she crossed the distance to stand between her lovers. Jaxson and Chase each stepped closer, wrapping an arm around Emma's waist to link them together.

"No, Dad. I'm not a distraction. I'm the glue that holds us all together."

Jaxson couldn't have described her role in their relationship better. He and Chase had been together for years, but it was only with Emma that their friendship had transformed to love.

Her father was still confused. "I don't understand. Which one is your boyfriend?"

"Daddy, please. Sit down."

"No."

Mrs. Fischer piped in. "Robert, Emma's right. You should sit." When he glanced her way with doubt, she added a stern, "Sit. Now."

Her husband moved on autopilot to pull out a chair from around the kitchen table and slide into it, a look of confused defeat on his face.

Within seconds, Emma's mother approached the threesome, first hugging her daughter before pulling Chase into a big hug. When she turned towards Jaxson, their eyes met and he saw her approval shining back at him. He hadn't expected her to take him in her arms too, hugging him tightly. A foreign homesickness for his own mother invaded and he realized it would be good to at least see her the following week, even if it meant putting up with his father.

When the hug ended she stayed close, addressing Jaxson directly, her hands on his chest. "My husband did me a favor when he stormed out of the diner. Emma finally opened up on the walk here and told me everything."

Jaxson's face must have betrayed some of the panic he felt at the thought of Mrs. Fischer knowing *everything* because she quickly stammered "Well almost everything.... Enough anyway..." clearly flustered.

Jaxson turned his mega-watt smile on her, relief at her acceptance sinking in.

Emma questioned her parent, "Wait. You're not mad mom?

The women turned to each other. "Mad? My goodness, no. I'm happy for you. All of you. All I want is for my baby to be happy and right now, it's easy to see these men are making that happen. I want you to travel... to see the world. Live your life. There is more than enough time to settle down and figure out the long term plan later." She paused, glancing back at Jaxson and Chase before finishing. "But, if you do anything to purposefully hurt my little girl... I'll hunt you down and castrate you. Understand?"

Jaxson didn't doubt her for one minute and loved that Emma's mother would go to the mat to protect her daughter, something his own mother had refused to do when confronted with her husband's will.

"You have my word, ma'am. That will never be necessary."

"That's good. And stop this ma'am stuff. I'm Linda."

"Linda? What the hell are you saying?" Emma's dad was still not up to speed.

"I'm saying these men make my daughter happy and that's the best present a mom can ask for."

"But, you don't understand. They're just using her to cover up their own relationship as a couple."

Jaxson jumped in to clarify. "But sir, you don't understand. I'm not with Chase. I'm with Chase *and* Emma. Together. There is no couple."

It took several long seconds for Mr. Fischer to finally work out what they were trying to say. As understanding dawned, he looked away from his daughter in confusion.

Jaxson couldn't really blame him. The relationship they had formed was the kind normally hidden behind closed doors, never to be discussed. With the men's high profile, the minute they stopped hiding out in an off-campus house in Madison, Wisconsin, they would put Emma at risk for public scrutiny and scorn.

The last thing he wanted to do was change her mind, but he just had to know. "So you really decided to come with us?" He heard the vulnerability in his voice.

Chase had gone to her again and was hugging her as she answered them. "I kept thinking about how sad I was when I got home from France without you. I regretted not staying in touch. My heart hurt when I thought I'd never see you again. If I'm honest, I'm still scared shitless I'm going to get hurt when you come to your senses and realize you settled for me when you could have any woman in the world, but I will never forgive myself if I don't give us a shot. I mean... you came for me. You took a month off for me. You stood up to Roberta for me. The least I can do is see what happens, right?"

He had to be careful, but he couldn't let it pass. "Emma. What have I told you about putting yourself down? That sounded a bit like you were still thinking you were somehow less deserving than others." He raised his eyebrow to get his point across, while his back was to her father. The rosy blush to her cheeks assured him she got his message loud and clear.

"I didn't mean... At least I didn't call myself fat this time. I just meant..."

Chase was hugging her, trying to help. "I think you should stop while you're ahead, sweetheart."

Emma's father sat at the kitchen table, silently taking it all in. He was no longer flushed. In fact, he looked pale as if he were in shock. The rest of the occupants of the room seemed oblivious to his distress. Jax wasn't sure it was a good idea, but he moved to the table, taking the seat across the table from the older man. He didn't register Jaxson immediately, too lost in his own thoughts.

Jaxson extended the olive branch first. "I know this is coming as a surprise, sir. I don't entirely blame you for your concerns. I can only try to reassure you that I really do have Emma's best interest at heart."

Gone was the man's anger. It took her father a long minute to reply as he processed his shock at the news of his daughter's unconventional relationship. By the time he spoke softly, what remained was loving concern. "What will happen to her when this doesn't work out after all?"

Jax knew that was a fair question. "I'm going to do all I can to make sure that Chase and I never hurt Emma, but no matter what happens in the long run, she will never want for anything the rest of her life."

"How can you promise that? She is giving up on her education."

"No, sir. She already has her undergrad degree and I will

encourage her to get her masters online. She'll be able to keep up with her education from anywhere on the globe."

"And how are her mother and I going to be able to see her? She used to visit every few weeks. Having her in France last year almost killed me. She's our only child." He looked so sad. "I'm going to miss her."

It was Emma that answered him, moving to sit next to her father. "Daddy, I may not be able to visit as often, but I'm sure I'll be able to fly home, right Jax?" She looked at him expectantly with hope in her eyes.

"Of course you can, Em. In fact, your parents can fly to visit you too. We'd love to have them come see the world with us."

He saw the tears threatening in her eyes at his generous offer. The funny thing was, he knew these were good people. He'd spent the bulk of his life surrounded by fakes and wannabes. He was still getting used to the fact that good people like the Fischers existed in the world. He genuinely looked forward to spending more time with them.

It was Mrs. Fischer who eased the awkward silence that had fallen over the kitchen. "Well I think we've stayed long enough. Let's get heading home, Robert. We need to stop and pick up some groceries. I'm hoping to see all three of you on Sunday."

Emma looked shocked. "But, Mom. You still want us all to come? I mean, Grandma will be there. And what if Mrs. Spinner spies on us from next door? I'm not good at lying and well...."

Linda walked back to talk directly to her daughter. "Listen to me, Emma. First, I'm not asking you or even wanting you to lie." She paused, collecting her thoughts. "Let me ask you a question. Do you really want this relationship to work with these men? I mean really work?"

"You know I do."

"So if you can't be proud of it with the people who love you most in the world, how exactly do you expect to go public? They are not truck drivers or schoolteachers. They are famous models.

There will be no hiding you from their fans for long. Don't you think your grandmother would rather you tell her in person than read about it in a tabloid or see it on the six o'clock news?"

Emma glanced nervously around the room, taking the temperature of all of the occupants... the people who truly did love her the most in the world.

"Okay, fine. You're right. We'll be there."

Once it was decided, Emma wasn't the only nervous one in the room. One look at Chase and Jaxson knew the men wouldn't be sleeping well, worried about what lay ahead of them on Sunday. They'd laid low long enough. It was time they took their relationship public.

CHAPTER 16

THEIR JOURNEY AS A TRIO

Shopping/Buy:
Haircut & Highlights
Mani-Pedi
Tanning salon
New wardrobe
Make-up/Make-over
Bathing suit and wrap
Brazilian wax
Suitcase

"WHAT THE HELL are you doing up at four in the morning, baby?" Emma almost jumped out of her skin as Jaxson's deep voice broke her concentration. His long fingers squeezed her tense shoulders, eliciting a surprised squeak. His gentle massaging motion did wonders towards relieving the growing tension that had been swirling like a tornado inside her.

"I couldn't sleep. I have too much on my mind. Ah... not quite so hard. That hurts."

"It hurts because you're wound tight. Let me work some of the kinks out."

Emma closed her eyes and let her chin drop to her chest as she tried to relax under Jaxson's ministrations. The pen she'd been holding too tightly slipped from her fingers as his technique moved to a light karate chop action across the taut muscle connecting her head and shoulders. The room was dark save the small lamp on the desk in front of her, illuminating the loose-leaf paper containing a brain-dump of all things panicking her at the moment.

Jaxson's magical hands worked wonders on her shoulders before trekking lower to slip into her worn terry robe to fondle her heavy breasts. It was then she remembered another important stop she needed to make at the mall—Victoria's Secret. If she was going to travel the world with sexy models, the least she could do is upgrade her undergarments from Target.

Her lover had obviously been looking over her shoulder. "What is all this and why did you need to get up in the middle of the night to write it?"

Emma used her left arm to cover the lists. She knew they were a glimpse into her own insecurities as much as anything else. When he reached for the paper, she self-consciously tried to flip the list over, but Jax was having none of it, picking up the top sheet as Emma groaned.

When Jax was quiet for a long minute, she started to shiver in spite of the room feeling oppressively stuffy. When the silence became awkward, she dared a peek over her shoulder to find a scowling Jaxson. He didn't look mad. He looked... alarmed.

"I can explain."

"Not even twenty-four hours. I'm an idiot. You really had me fooled." The flat defeat in his voice was new.

"Excuse me? I have no idea what you mean."

He struggled to find the right words. When he did, Emma's heart raced faster.

"How ironic. One of the things I adored about you is that none of this kind of shit was important to you. I loved the real you, not some fake painted version trying to hide yourself. And what's the first thing you do when you decide to come with us? Plan to turn yourself into a cookie cutter version of exactly what I'm trying to distance myself from. New hair... tan... clothes... nails..."

The venom in his voice stabbed deep, wounding her. She hadn't missed his use of past tense either. *Adored. Loved.* Like it was over.

The little voice she'd been shouting down for weeks was back. It had been whispering she wasn't worthy of the two extraordinary men but now it was shouting 'I told you so' in her ear as she fought to stay calm.

It was Emma's turn to struggle for the right words to answer his accusation. She felt his anger growing as she fumbled, frightened how things could blow up so spectacularly in the matter of minutes.

She had loved every single minute of her time with the men as they'd all played hide and seek with the rest of the world in her run-down attic. Safe from prying eyes and judgmental commentary that was sure to focus on how insane it was to try to go public with a ménage relationship with two famous sex-gods.

She had dreaded the day it would end. She'd hoped they could make it at least a few months. Even she thought they'd make it more than a few hours.

Righteous anger consumed her. She pushed to her feet, knocking the desk chair over to crash against the wood floor as she turned on her lover, ripping the list from his hand.

"You have some nerve, Jaxson. What is so objectionable about this list?" He started to interrupt her, but once she got started, she was on a roll.

She was vaguely aware of Chase moving into her peripheral view as she got up in Jaxson's face. "Do you have any idea how scared shitless I am to leave this house with you tomorrow? Do you have a fucking clue how much the media is going to crucify me when they get the first pictures of us together? I can see the headlines now. 'A-lister hunks go slumming and pick up chunky co-ed.'" Emma crumpled the list while waving it like a flag in his face, her voice shouting. "So, yeah. I want to get my hair done and maybe buy an outfit that isn't a college T-shirt and jeans. Forgive me if I want to try to look the best I can before the cameras start rolling. You may not care what the tabloids print about me, and while I will never be able to compete with the gorgeous models you're surrounded by every day, I'd like to at least try not to embarrass you or myself by looking like a frumpy BBW."

Emma could see the array of emotions flitting through Jaxson's eyes throughout her monologue. She'd never spoken to him in even close to that tone, but dammit he hurt her.

Chase had come behind her, wrapping his arms around her waist, trying to pull her away from the steaming Jaxson, but Emma slapped him away. Jax was stunned into silence and she took the opportunity to pile on. "And for your information, that wasn't the first list I got up to make. I was lying in bed, unable to sleep because of all of the things I need to get done before I can leave here with you. You guys may be on vacation and having fun playing video games between sex marathons, but I'm still working, and teaching, and trying to wrap up my classes. Now I have to add moving to the mix. I'm a little stressed and quite honestly, I'd appreciate a little help." She reached to her left, grabbing the second sheet of paper and shoving it in Jaxson's face. When he wouldn't take it, she started reading it off to him.

To Do List:
Pack stuff up to take to Mom & Dad's for storage
Call Professor Kanowski to cancel last classes
Finish global economics paper
Pass off research notes to study group

Transfer money to pay rent
Turn in global monetary project
Tell housemates I'm leaving
Return library books
Pick-up birth control prescription at pharmacy

"DOES that sound like the list of some maniac only interested in taking advantage of you and your fame?"

Chase reached out again, pulling her close, her back to his naked chest as he leaned in to coax her down from the ledge. "It's gonna be okay, honey. We'll help you with anything you need. I'm sure Jaxson just misunderstood."

Chase's soothing rocking had just started to help calm her when Jaxson finally found his voice.

"Emma, I owe you an apology about the lists. I was wrong to jump to conclusions and I'm sorry about that. I'm even sorry that I didn't pick up on how stressed you were getting, but..."

Sweet relief. He'd apologized. It meant so much to her that he'd admit when he was wrong. She had just started to catch her breath when the sharp edge to his voice returned, anger flaring hot in his eyes.

"But I'm pretty sure I've made it very clear that I will not allow you to put yourself down or call yourself names. If you have insecurities or concerns, you bring them to us and we'll talk through them. We don't hide them under the rug or worse yet, slap a layer of makeup and new wardrobe on and think it's gonna fix anything. Trust me on this. That's a slippery slope."

Her anger was ebbing, the adrenalin in her bloodstream diluting. In its wake was fear. Fear of being ridiculed. Worse yet, publicly judged. But she'd given it lots of thought and the only thing she could think of that was worse than being crucified by the media was being alone again after sampling how joyous life could be in the arms of not one, but two remarkable men. She knew with every fiber of her being that she'd regret it for the rest of her life if she let them leave Madison without her.

But that meant she was actually going to have to leave the safety of the attic. It also meant she was going to have to apologize to the angry man in front of her. Not for her outburst. Not even for her feelings of inadequacy, but for not trusting him to listen to her worries.

"Fine. I'm sorry I yelled at you."

"Seriously? That's all you've got?"

She knew what he was waiting for, but she also knew she'd been punished for saying much less before. She could feel the skin on her ass tingling in anticipation of the spanking she knew was in her near future.

"Alright, maybe I should have told you how scared shitless I am to leave the house with you. That I'm pretty sure people will burst out laughing when they see you with me. How social media is going to light up. We'll be trending on Twitter within an hour and the focus of a scathing TMZ exposé within twenty-four hours."

Shut the fuck up, Emma. You're making it worse.

The scowl on Jaxson's face turned darker as he stepped up to sandwich her between the two men. His hands squeezed her biceps as Chase's fingers dug into her hips, each holding her stationary.

"Look at me, Emma."

She'd trained her eyes on his adam's apple directly in front of her to avoid seeing the disappointment in his eyes.

"Now, Emma." His order had her snapping to attention.

She'd expected anger, but she saw a sadness in Jax's eyes. She held her breath waiting for him to bust her for putting herself down.

"I owe you another apology. I was so happy to just hide out for a while that it didn't dawn on me that you were afraid to leave. I'll fix that tomorrow. We're gonna tackle that list of yours together and by the end of the day, you'll know that all of your fears were unfounded."

She was smart enough not to laugh at what was surely a joke. It was a good thing too since his next words were scary enough.

"Now what do you think is going to happen next?"

She held her breath, afraid to say the words.

"Emma, answer me. What happens when you put yourself down?"

Her answer was barely audible. "You spank me."

"No. I spanked you the last time. I see it didn't take."

This was not good. What was worse than a spanking?

"Chase, go grab some rope and the wooden paddle. Emma is about to get her first paddling. We'll see if that makes a more lasting impression on our girl."

Emma's legs felt wobbly under her as Chase released her and stepped away to follow Jaxson's order. He was back entirely too fast. She snuck a glance up at her Dom and saw his jaw locked with determination.

This was very bad. Her heart raced with fear, guilt and excitement. How she could be excited to feel the paddle was a mystery, but the vibration in her pussy could not be denied.

Jaxson released her left arm and pulled her back towards the desk in front of the lone window. He turned her to face the flat surface and stripped her of her old terry robe, leaving her naked. The desk lamp illuminated her heavy breasts for any passer-by coming home late from a night of partying.

The touch of his palm pressing her to lean over the back of the straight-backed chair gave a brief relief to hide from voyeurs, until she saw Chase kneeling on one side of the chair and Jax on the other, each securing her hands to the front legs. She was able to grasp onto the side rungs of the chair, but her lower tummy then pressed into the top of backrest uncomfortably.

She truly panicked as they pulled her legs wide to the outside of the chair, securing her ankles to the back legs and rendering her incapacitated. They worked silently, solemn in their solidarity to teach her a lesson. She thought about begging them to stop. About apologizing. But she knew it would do no good. Hell, she wasn't even sure if yelling *puppies*, her safeword, would get her out of the punishment coming.

They left her there for what seemed an eternity. She couldn't see them. She could only hear small sounds across the room. Whispers as the men plotted her doom.

Chase was next to her then, his palm connecting with her ass that was displayed perfectly for their pleasure and her pain. His hand spanking wasn't particularly hard or painful, but he was thorough, peppering her entire bare ass until she knew she had to be glowing with heat. She bit back the tears threatening to fall, knowing this wasn't even the main attraction.

When Chase finished her warm up, he stepped back to make way for Jaxson. She sensed him behind and to her left. She felt the cool wood as he brushed it against her warm bottom. A whimper got away from her, sounding pitiful in the otherwise quiet attic.

"I'm not looking forward to this, Emma. You understand this is not going to be a fun, sexy, playful spanking?"

Surely that was a rhetorical question. When he prodded her with the edge of the paddle, she knew she'd thought wrong. "Yes, sir."

"Chase and I have devised a punishment that's gonna help you remember how much we love you all day tomorrow when we are out and about."

That didn't sound good.

"Chase, you count for our girl. I have a feeling she's going to have a little trouble concentrating tonight."

"Yes, sir." She couldn't bear to look at Chase. He sounded as afraid as she felt. That couldn't be a good sign.

Emma had just rested her forehead on the seat of the wood chair when the first crack of wood hitting flesh went off in the room like a firecracker. The heavy thud penetrated deep. She almost missed Chase's count of one due to her own groan of pain.

The second swat was worse—much worse. The paddle was so big that two strikes were all it took to cover her entire bottom. She clenched and unclenched her flaming cheeks, desperate to rub away the ache, but helpless to do anything but wait for the next punishing swat.

"Oh, God!" She couldn't hold in her cry when the third hard swat crossed over the middle of her ass. The agony went so deep that she was sure she would be bruised when it was over. Tears spilled out of her, droplets falling to the wooden chair. "Please... no more. That's enough. I've learned my lesson."

Her lovers answered her with the next heavy swing of the paddle. Chase cried out "four" as he knelt next to the chair and reached to stroke the back of her head gently, trying to bring her comfort. His loving caresses helped her know he cared, but did nothing to alleviate the searing fire burning up her buttocks.

She was sobbing by the time Chase cried out "six." His hand had moved to caress her back.

Surely that was enough.

"You are doing well, Emma. Only four more to go."

"No, no, no... please."

Number seven was the hardest yet because he didn't just deliver the paddle, but the lecture began. "Tell me again why you are being punished, Emma."

He thought she could form words? It took her a minute to calm her crying enough to sob out, "Because I put myself down."

"Eight!" Chase's counting was getting louder as Jaxson's swings built up power. "That's right. I don't appreciate you saying hurtful things about the woman I love."

"Nine!"

She was going to die. She was sure of it. Surely her big old ass was going to fall off it throbbed so hard. It was around the count of nine that she realized that her clit was throbbing just as intensely. Christ, she couldn't wait for Jaxson to fuck her. He always fucked her after a punishment. It would almost be worth getting to...

"Ten!" The crack that filled the room sounded different and her own scream of pain drowned out the sound of Jax throwing the wooden paddle to the floor. He had landed her final strike lower, coming up from below to connect with her tender sit spot where her ass met her thighs. She was going to feel that one for days.

Emma was too lost in her own little world where she retreated to figuratively lick her wounds. It wasn't until she felt her lovers brushing against her body that she started to calm her tears.

Chase was in front of her. She smelled his distinctive masculine scent as he stroked her long hair. She sniffled loudly, knowing she had to be a hot mess of snot and tears.

She gasped as she felt Jaxson brush up against her bare ass, reigniting the pain that was throbbing.

"You've made it through part one of your punishment. Only two more parts to go."

She had to hear him wrong. Her ass couldn't take any more. It would fall off. Emma panicked and started struggling again to free her hands or legs, but Chase's caresses stilled her. He crouched in front of her to hold a tissue up to her nose. "Blow for me, baby."

He didn't bother to wipe her tears away, but instead, stood and stepped closer, lifting her head so she had to look up just in time for him to slide his iron-like cock between her lips, thrusting to the back of her throat and cutting off her breath.

"Eyes, Emma." Chase loved to have her look into his eyes as he fucked her mouth. She saw his dominance warring with lust as he rode her throat, stopping occasionally to let her gasp for a breath. She'd been conditioned to love giving him a blowjob because it almost always came accompanied with Jaxson filling her pussy.

Only tonight it wasn't the touch of his erection to her lady parts she felt. It was the cold dribble of something wet between her ass cheeks, dripping onto her puckered bottom hole.

Oh God, surely he wasn't going to take her there. Emma still wasn't sure how she felt about anal sex. She couldn't say she hated it, but she certainly didn't love it. Sure, she found it emotionally powerful when both men were inside her together, filling her completely.

Jaxson was being rougher than normal tonight, thrusting one and then two fingers in a couple of times at the same tempo Chase filled her throat.

"In case you haven't figured it out, the next phase of your punishment is going to be getting fucked in your tight little hole by not just me, but by Chase as well. We're going to ride you until you are sore enough that you'll be thinking of us all day tomorrow. Every time you sit. Every time you brush up against something with your cute little bottom. You'll be reminded of what happens to naughty little girls who put themselves down. Do you understand?"

She had no idea how he expected her to answer with Chase buried in her mouth like a stellar gag. The tip of Jaxson's engorged dick dragged up and down the cleft of her ass, teasing her pucker with small jabs that stretched the entrance to her anus wide before receding.

Emma closed her eyes, afraid it was going to hurt when Jaxson pressed inside. She didn't feel ready.

"Eyes, Emma. I want to watch as he fucks you." She wanted to hate what was about to happen, but unmistakable excitement and love poured out for the men taking her in hand.

Jaxson always called the shots so Chase's order surprised her. "Fuck her now, Jaxson. Show her what we think of her putting herself down."

His thrust was swift and hard, not the gentle handling of a lover, but the power of a Dom. Chase dragged his eyes away from Emma's to look up at his best friend. Emma watched as the men each leaned forward to kiss above her while they stilled, each buried deep inside her body.

When the kiss ended, the real fucking began. The men rode her hard, bodies slapping against flesh at a punishing rate.

"Don't you dare come yet, Chase. You have another job to do tonight."

That was cryptic. "Yes, sir."

"And Emma, you will not be allowed to come for the next twenty-four hours. If you're a good girl, I might let you come tomorrow night."

She was happy she couldn't have answered if she wanted to. Jaxson's erection plowed into her ass again and again, stretching her uncomfortably as he chased his pleasure. Chase had to stop several times deep in her mouth, she assumed to avoid shooting his load.

The final minute of her buggering was intense. Jaxson drove into her harder and faster, pulling her to him with his hands gripping her hips and riding her until he cried out his pleasure, shooting hot cum deep into her bowels.

The pressure of Jaxson's weight leaning across her back took her breath away and then he was gone allowing her to gasp for precious air. The men traded places and only then did she want to stop their game. The word *puppy* was on the tip of her tongue as she felt Chase's thick cock announcing its arrival at her already sore bottom hole. He'd never taken her in the ass before.

"Please, no. You're too big."

"Shhh. I'm not going to hurt you. Only teach you a lesson."

At least he filled her slowly, giving her body time to adjust to his girth. He hadn't put on any additional lube, using the cum oozing out of her body that Jax had just deposited as natural lubrication.

It took him a few minutes of shallow insertions to finally open her up wide enough to take his whole cock inside her. It felt so good and so bad. It made her want him to reach around and frig her pussy that had to be dripping, but he grabbed her hips instead and started pounding into her as hard as Jaxson had before him.

This time she didn't have a cock in her mouth to stop her from crying out. "Please... I need to come too. Touch my pussy, Chase. Please!"

Jaxson was crouched in front of her lifting her chin to look him in the eyes through her tears. "That's a good girl. Take your punishment. You get to service us with your tight little pucker without coming. Just wait until you see what the grand finale is going to be."

In that moment, she couldn't care less. The burning of her ass-fucking was consuming her, lighting her on fire as Chase thundered in and out hard and fast. She felt truly punished by the time he shouted his climax and deposited his load deep inside her to co-mingle with Jaxson's spunk.

Like her other lover before him, he leaned down over her, placing his chest to her back and holding onto her as he crushed her. Her legs and wrists hurt from her pulling to be free. Chase remained snaked inside her as he caught his breath.

Emma lay helplessly waiting for her lovers to release her, not sure if the external or internal part of her butt hurt worse. She vaguely registered Jaxson leaving her. He returned a minute later to stand behind her next to Chase.

"Okay, pull out."

She breathed a sigh of relief when her body cavity was finally her own, but it was short lived. Emma felt a hardness returning to the entrance to her well-ridden asshole.

"Relax, Emma. This plug isn't quite as big as our Chase. It's gonna fill you quite nicely, though."

She was already so sore that it burned as he pushed the wide flange of the hard sex toy past the ring of her bottom hole, shoving it home as she yelped. Thankfully the flared end of the plug wasn't as wide, giving some relief to the entrance to her anus.

"Oh, please. It's too big. Take it out. It doesn't feel good." She had started to wriggle as hard as she could with no effect.

"I'm glad to hear it. It's a punishment. It's a reminder of how important you are to us. Not to mention, I love the idea that the plug is trapping Chase's and my seed deep inside you together. You'll carry us around with you until we allow you to expel us."

He was devious, but the idea of having their cum buried inside her bottom did excite her. As much as she hated the pain, she always felt closer to the men after being disciplined. The phenomenon had confused her at first, but she'd decided that her punishments were just as intimate an act as was having sex.

The men finally released her from the restraints and both helped her stand. Each man took a wrist. Their gentle rubbing where the ropes had cut into her were in direct conflict with the harsh punishment they'd dished out minutes before.

Jaxson scooped her into his arms to carry her the few feet back to their bed. The cool sheets almost scorched her bottom and she scrambled to quickly roll to her side to get the pressure off her disciplined ass.

The men cocooned her, climbing into bed on either side of her and trapping her between them in an intimate pile of co-mingled arms and legs.

The hardness shoved up her back hole was unforgiving, refusing to let her forget its presence as her lovers snuggled her. It was a strange reminder of how kinky their little trio was and yet, she wouldn't change it for the world.

It didn't take long for Emma to become drowsy, thinking about how strange it was that the painful paddling had done exactly what she'd needed... relaxed her enough to let sleep become a possibility. Unfortunately, knowing that tomorrow they would take their relationship public weighed on her. She drifted into a fitful sleep filled with nightmares brought on by her insecurities.

CHAPTER 17

She awoke to hands groping her. She was horny as hell and the fingers stroking her bare folds weren't pressing hard enough to get her off. Palms cupped her heavy breasts while fingers probed her pussy, brushing against her clit lightly. Lovingly. Teasing.

Her voice cracked as she begged, "Yes... harder."

The fingers disappeared immediately. She opened her eyes to find two stern men peering down at her. "Time to rise and shine, baby. We have a big day today."

She groaned as memories of her middle-of-the-night punishment returned and she was sure she had to be blushing. As if to drive their message home, Jaxson pulled at the butt plug still lodged deep inside her, pulling it out just far enough to ensure the widest part of the toy rested exactly at her opening, stretching her uncomfortably.

"Take it out. Please," she whined.

"Sorry, baby. Not until later. Much later."

"But... I thought you said we were going out today."

"Yep, all four of us. You, me, Chase and that little hitchhiker shoved up where the sun doesn't shine."

"Oh, God. No. Not out in public. What if..."

"You'll ask permission if you have to go to the bathroom." Chase replied much too cheerfully.

"Seriously?" She'd never dreamed they'd try to dominate her bodily functions. How mortifying.

"Seriously. Chase, why don't you take our girl and help her shower and get ready for our day. I have a few phone calls I need to make before we leave."

The dull soreness across her ass flared to an uncomfortable ache as she rolled over to climb out of bed. She scrambled to her feet to take the pressure off. She had grown accustomed to their near constant nakedness when in the bedroom together, but today she felt more vulnerable before the men. She'd unloaded a lot of her undeclared insecurities on them in the middle of the night, and despite the pain of her punishment, there was a part of her that was relieved it was out in the open.

Chase held out her robe for her to slide into as he put on a pair of boxers to make the trek down to the outdated bathroom on the floor below.

"You don't need to help me down, you know. My ass may be sore, but I think I can make it on my own."

Chase grinned. "Maybe, but you're on all day punishment. That means the plug doesn't come out and no self-pleasure in the shower, little girl."

Christ. He'd read her mind. She had totally hoped to get off in the shower to help take the edge off. She'd never be able to make it through the day without embarrassing herself if she didn't.

"How...?"

They'd arrived in the small room and he took the time to lock the door before he turned to pin her with a dominant gaze that only made her sexual need worse.

"Baby, we know you better than you seem to think we do, although I admit, you surprised me with your little tirade last night. Not that Jaxson didn't deserve it because he did. I'm just warning you that the only reason he stopped at ten instead of fifty last night was because he feels guilty for not recognizing the stress you've been under."

"Fifty? I'd die."

"Nope, but you may wish you had. Trust me. I've only had to survive it once. Fifty swats of Jaxson's paddle may not kill you, but it makes you want to die for a little while."

"What the hell did you do to deserve such a severe punishment?"

He hesitated and she wondered if he was going to answer her.

"I guess you deserve to know since... well... it has to do with how Jaxson and my relationship changed from just friends to lovers."

Instead of starting the story, he led her to the toilet. "I'll start the shower. I'll fill you in while I wash you and your hair."

"But... I need to pee."

Chase's smirked. "I kinda figured. Hurry 'cause I need to go too."

"You mean..."

"Baby, we're gonna travel the world together. Live together. Sleep and eat together. And yes, share one bathroom."

He made her feel like an innocent. She pushed down her insecurity and did her business while Chase brushed his teeth and then they traded places.

Once they were under the spray of the hot water, her lover started his story as he lathered her long hair, massaging her scalp lovingly as he shared his own intimate memories.

"It was almost two years ago now I guess. We were in LA for a shoot and some promotional gigs. Jax and I had been growing closer and closer, but neither of us had acknowledged that our friendship felt like it was changing. I think we were both confused about the growing attraction we had for each other, especially since both of us had a pretty steady stream of women coming and going at that point."

Emma worked to push down the jealously that reared up listening to her lover talk so casually about sleeping with so many others before her.

Chase continued, unaware his words had given her pause. "It was a Friday night. I'd begged Jaxson to go out dancing with me. I was restless, needing something, not knowing what. He refused saying he was tired so I went out alone. I went to a trendy club and right away had a crowd hitting on me. It was the first time..."

He paused so long she looked over her shoulder at him. She couldn't read the expression on his face. "Chase?"

He smiled then, a sad, apologetic smile that confused her. "I was an idiot that night, Em. I drank too much. Popped a few pills someone gave me. I never even knew what they were. I had sex with a couple women in a dark corner of the club. I didn't even get their names. I was about to leave when this really hot guy came up and started hitting on me. I'd been feeling closer to Jaxson, but we'd never acted on it and in my stupor of the night, I thought it might be a good idea to try the whole same-sex thing with the hottie who seemed to want me."

Emma knew Chase enough to know that something bigger than his first gay encounter had happened that night. She was patient, enjoying his massages to her scalp, moving down to her shoulders, soapy hands on her breasts, tummy, hips... his hands were everywhere and she loved it.

He continued when he was ready. "He took me to his apartment that wasn't far from the club. The second I got there I knew I was in trouble. As soon as he locked the door, he turned and grabbed me, kissing me brutally. At first, it was passionate, but then he bit my lip hard enough to make it bleed. All I could think about was that I had a shoot the next day and Roberta was gonna kick my ass.

"Then the real fun started. He started stripping me in the living room. We never made it to a bed. At first I went along, but when he shoved me to my knees and jammed his dick down my throat so far I almost threw up things went from bad to worse. Keep in mind I was drunk and wasted. I tried to fight him off but... shit he was strong."

Emma's heart raced. Her Chase had been raped. She knew it and it broke her heart. She turned and hugged him hard, hanging on to him as the hot water sluiced over their soapy bodies. She didn't need him to say any more, but he went on with his story anyway, his voice a monotone of steadiness that told her he was repeating it on auto-pilot, trying not to internalize his words.

"He kept me there until morning. He fucked me so hard I bled. I had bruises all over from where he'd restrained me with force. I remember thinking how pissed Jaxson was going to be. In my insecurities, I thought it would be because I'd screwed up the shoot. When I took a cab back to the hotel early in the morning, I went straight to his room. I still remember collapsing into his arms as soon as he opened the door. I'd held it together pretty well until then, but as soon as I saw the horror on his face as he realized how fucked up I was I burst out crying like a little girl.

"That was the day he changed from my friend to my Dom. It took weeks for me to heal physically, but our relationship changed forever that day. He was furious I'd put myself in danger. That I'd gone with a stranger. I was a hot mess. I needed his dominance so much that I think in some ways, I'd been purposefully taking risks to get his attention. That night was the first time we talked about me handing over control to him. Ironically, I think he was most angry that he wouldn't get to be my first... well, you know. He lost it when he found out the asshole hadn't even used condoms. He'd fucked me bareback.

"In spite of the trauma I'd gone through, it felt so damn good to have Jax taking care of me. One night a few weeks later, as soon as I'd healed from the shit the asshole had done to me, Jaxson got out the paddle and told me it was time to learn my lesson about personal safety. He paddled my ass raw that night, lecturing me the whole time about how important I was. About how I was never to put myself in danger like that again. When it was over, he scooped me into his arms and he sat and rocked me while I cried. He reassured me that all was forgiven and then he kissed me. I mean really kissed me and I'm pretty sure I've loved him since that minute. It just took us awhile to admit it. We still didn't start making love until months later.

"Jaxson insisted on taking me to the doctor every month for blood tests to make sure I hadn't contracted some shitty disease. What I hated the most about those doctor's visits was that he would paddle me again before we left for the doctor so I'd have a reminder as I sat there getting blood drawn about exactly why I was there.

"It was the night of the last test when I'd gotten my six month clean bill of health that he drove me home to his apartment in New York City. The second we got in the apartment we were all over each other. It was like someone had shot a gun at the start of a race. We both just knew it was time. We didn't leave his bedroom for a couple of days, kinda like how we've been hanging out here with you."

Emma had listened quietly, patiently, as Chase shared the important story with her. A part of her brain told her she should feel like an outsider in the threesome. That she was intruding in the men's love affair, but in her heart, she believed what Jaxson had told her over and over. Emma was the glue the men needed to hold them together.

"So, why didn't you guys just stick together after that?"

"We tried for a little while, but we were honest with each other. We were both still attracted to women. Neither of us was ready to really settle down or go public and have to deal with the fallout."

That alarmed her. "But... well then why are you going to go public now? Aren't you still worried?"

He cupped her face as water fell on their shoulders, splashing stray drops of water.

"Honey, we're ready now because you're here. Because for the first time we found someone that makes us feel whole. I know it's weird because Jax and I have been having sex now for over a year, but I've never considered myself gay. Not that there is anything wrong with that, because there's not. I just knew it was more complicated than that. It took us some experimentation to figure it all out."

She wanted to press him more, but the water was starting to get cool. The old house's plumbing was sub-standard.

"Now, let's get you rinsed off and out of here. We have a busy day ahead."

"But, can't you just give me one little..."

The crack of his palm connecting with her wet ass was so fast she didn't have time to prepare.

"Jaxson said no. I said no. Don't press me, little girl or we'll extend your punishment another day."

"Meanie."

"Yeah, well Jax may be our Dom, but I'm the switch of this little family. You'll behave or feel my belt on that cute little ass of yours."

"Not fair! Who do I get to be a Domme for?"

"We'll be sure to get you a puppy when we settle down."

Her heart constricted with love and hope. How she prayed they'd be together long enough to settle down with the two men who'd turned her life upside-down.

* * *

AN HOUR LATER, they were settling into a large booth at the same diner she'd been to the day before with her parents. The same waitress greeted her with a smile.

"Welcome back. Looks like you've upgraded your dining partners today."

Emma grinned. "I sure did. I'll take a coffee and OJ please."

As the waitress retreated with all three of their orders, Jaxson commented, "See, we are in public and the sky isn't falling."

"Yeah, well the day is young." He sent her a cautionary look, his eyebrow raised in a way that made her ass tingle from the paddling the night before. As she wriggled in her seat the end of the anal plug pressed farther into her bottom, reminding her of her continued punishment.

Breakfast was uneventful until the waitress dropped off their check, filling their cups one last time with coffee.

"It took me awhile to place you, but aren't you guys the models I see in advertisements everywhere?"

Emma's heart raced, but the men took the question in stride, having years of practice being famous.

"That would be us."

"Wow, what brings you to Madison? Are you lucky enough to be their sister?" She pinned Emma with an envious stare.

Chase's hand was on her knee under the table. She felt him squeeze her as her eyes locked with Jaxson's across the table. The men were silent and she knew what they waited for.

Emma stumbled her way through the explanation. "Actually, I'm not their sister. I'm their..." She paused, her heart pumping with excitement as she looked at the waitress and finished with a confident, "girlfriend."

Shock flew through the older woman's expression. "Which one?"

Emma held her stare as she replied, "both."

The server looked back and forth between the men as if she expected them to protest, but Chase instead moved his arm around the back of the bench seat, pulling Emma closer to him to kiss the top of her head as Jaxson leaned forward to hold her hand that had just put down her coffee cup.

"Holy shit. You're one lucky girl."

Emma smiled shyly. "Yes. Yes, I am."

After she'd left, the men prodded her. "See, that wasn't so bad."

Emma had to agree. Maybe she'd made a mountain out of a molehill.

Their stop at the pharmacy had the men filling the cart with embarrassing products. They took the opportunity to stock up on lube and even an enema bag. She tried not to think about when they might try to use that.

When they got to the pharmacy counter to pick up her birth control pills, the pharmacist offered to check them out at the back register. She saw the elderly man eyeing up the men who stayed close on each side of her. It was clear to anyone who was watching there was something special about the threesome who couldn't seem to keep their hands off each other. With each item Chase stacked on the counter to be scanned, the more judgmental the pharmacist became, going as far as clucking disapproval at the lube.

Would this be how everyone over the age of twenty-five would react to their relationship? It didn't seem to bother the men so she tried to push her insecurity down.

The grocery store was next. They were out of everything at the house, but they also wouldn't be staying in Madison much longer. They took the time to go up and down every aisle, pointing out their favorite foods and snacks to each other and filling their cart with necessities like breakfast cereal, milk, and the makings for sandwiches. When they got to the fresh produce area, the men filled the cart with healthy fruits and vegetables.

Chase admitted, "I've gained ten pounds in the last few weeks just hanging out eating fast food, carry out and junk food. Roberta is gonna kick my ass if I don't lose a few before London."

"Yeah, well the only way I haven't gained the same is I've been running every other day at least. You need to get out and run."

Emma listened to their good-natured ribbing with annoyance. "So why is it you guys get to talk about needing to lose weight and I don't?"

Jaxson's hand on her ass stilled her as he leaned in to whisper into her ear, "Because we aren't body shaming ourselves or each other like you do."

She didn't get a chance to reply before a loud screech was heard behind them.

"Oh my God, it really is them! I heard rumors they were hanging around campus, but I didn't believe it." A busty blonde and raunchy red-head pushed into their personal space to sidle up to Jaxson, despite him still holding Emma's ass in his hand possessively. "Jaxson Davidson! Can I get your picture and an autograph?"

He squeezed Emma's ass, his subtle message to her to remain calm as Chase stepped forward to push between the women and Jaxson.

"Hello ladies. Let's take it down a notch. I don't think they heard you across campus yet."

"Chase Cartwright, too! You are even hotter in person! I love your hair longer like this." Emma wanted to bitch-slap the ballsy blonde who had dared to reach out and run her fingers through Chase's hair as if she had every right to touch him.

Did women really act like this?

Chase handled her beautifully, pulling her hand from his space and returning it deliberately to her own side, yet she was oblivious to his hint because she dug into her purse and came out with a pen. Emma watched in awe as she pulled her skimpy tank top aside to bare the ample swell of breast while she pressed the pen into Chase's hand.

"I'm out of paper, but you can give me an autograph on my body. In fact, you can do whatever you want to me, anywhere you want, if you get my drift."

Emma was actually embarrassed for the brash woman currently making a fool of herself, but she was also alarmed because her loud voice had begun to attract a crowd. Jaxson's hand moved from her ass up to wind around her waist, pulling her closer to his body making it clear she was with him.

The redhead wasn't interested in Chase. She was pouting as she noticed Jaxson cozying up to Emma. The sour look on her face matched her poisonous words when she opened her big mouth. "A man like you... believe me, you can do a bit better in the hook up department. Take me for example. I'm available."

Emma felt her Dom's muscles tightening as he fought to control his temper. Their first foray into public was turning out to be just about as disastrous as she'd predicted. The crowd was growing. People had their cell phones out, some whispering and pointing, others pressing forward to try to get a better look.

Jaxson turned to Emma and hugged her to him, whispering in her ear, "I'm sorry, baby. I'm gonna deal with this and then we'll get out of here." He kissed her forehead tenderly before releasing her, nodding to Chase who moved to take his place with Emma while Jaxson stepped closer to the two women who had started the scene.

A look of victory lit up the makeup-caked face of the blonde as Jaxson stepped close, invading her personal space for a change. Her look of victory didn't last long. He spoke into her ear too softly for Emma to hear his words, but whatever he said replaced victory with anger. She opened her mouth to argue with him, but he put his index finger against her lips and warned her. "Not another word. Turn around and get the hell away from us now, before I call the police and report you for harassment."

The women stomped off, cussing Jaxson out loudly as they left.

"Sorry for the disruption everyone. You can all go back to your shopping now. There's nothing to see here."

A college co-ed that had been taping the event on her phone looked like she might attempt to ask for an autograph, but then thought better of it as she glanced at the two departing women.

Only after the dust settled did Emma realize she was shaking. She wasn't sure if it was the too-cold air-conditioning or the too-hot embarrassment of the scene that had just played out. Regardless, Chase and Jaxson sandwiched her as they often did, all linked intimately until she started to feel better.

"Well, that was fun." Chase said, a bit too cheery.

Emma bit her tongue to keep from saying 'I told you so.' This was exactly the kind of reception she'd known she'd get when going into public with the gorgeous men she was in love with and they hadn't left Madison, Wisconsin yet. What was it going to be like in London or Paris, or God-forbid in Washington DC the following week when they went to the fund-raiser with Jaxson's family?

"Can we go home now, please?" She asked quietly. She wasn't sure whose hand was caressing her back, but it was helping.

Jaxson took charge as usual. "We aren't going to let a few idiots ruin our day. Let's get going to checkout."

They piled the groceries into the back of the rental truck and then drove Emma around campus running errand after errand, checking things off her list. With each checkmark she made, she felt another weight being lifted off her shoulders. By the time Jaxson pulled into the large mall on the outskirts of town she was downright floating. Other than the embarrassing event in the grocery store, the day had been fun—perfect even.

But she was tired and more than anything, she needed to get home so she could get rid of the hitchhiker still lodged in her ass. It had now been there for twelve hours and was becoming more uncomfortable by the minute. It didn't help that they'd insisted she eat a late lunch with them.

She tried one more time to dissuade the men from their current mission; operation Emma makeover.

"Can't we please go home now? I'm really tired. I didn't sleep well last night. We can come back tomorrow."

"That's enough, Emma. We are going to be busy taking some of your stuff to your parents tomorrow. We won't stay long, but I do want to get started on that big 'ole list of yours." Jaxson was authoritative as always.

The mall was cool in the July heat. It looked like it was a popular destination for others trying to cool off.

Emma tried not to notice the attention they were attracting as the threesome walked hand-in-hand window shopping, stopping to peruse through a few clothes stores before finally arriving at Victoria's Secret. The wolfish grins on the men's faces as they pulled her deeper into the store was almost worth the uncomfortable feelings she had looking at the stick-thin mannequins in their skimpy size two unmentionables. The men deserted her to spread out, each gathering up armfuls of sexy garments they couldn't wait for her to try on.

Emma meandered aimlessly, trying not to panic at the thought that the store may not have size sixteen anything and in her experience, a size sixteen in a place like this might fit a normal size six since things were cut so small.

Two beautiful store clerks were nearby gossiping, never bothering to offer to assist Emma, which suited her just fine. Yet, she watched with interest as the two young women noticed Jaxson and Chase talking nearby, holding up a sexy baby-doll negligee that was completely transparent. Emma blushed at the thought of wearing that for her men.

The urge to go to the ladies room was growing, pushing her into a submissive mindset as she realized she'd need permission from her Dom before she could do something as basic as use the restroom.

The sound of high-pitched giggles dragged her attention back to the store and she glanced over just in time to see the two workers trying their best to seduce her men. Their body language screamed 'fuck me' and their annoying voices carried across the space, grating on Emma.

Jaxson looked over and caught her eye, smiling the sexiest smile in his arsenal of sexy. It disarmed her completely. That man —that sex-god—he loved her. That the grinning hunk next to him loved her too blew her mind. Her heart contracted with love just as her bottom contracted in cramps. She reached for her gurgling tummy and both men's smiles waned with worry.

She hadn't heard what had been discussed before, but when the men got to her side and stopped, she witnessed the surprised looks on the faces of the two sales associates. They turned green with envy as the men held her, excitedly showing her what they'd picked out for her to try on.

Chase was like a little boy. "Look at this awesome robe. It will be a perfect replacement for your current one."

"Hey, there is nothing wrong with my robe."

Jaxson snorted. "Not if this was 1950. Sorry babe, but the old-lady robe has to go."

The word robe was generous to describe the scrap of cloth Chase held up for her inspection. "Where's the rest of it?"

"This could be your summer robe, for when it's really hot."

"I can't wait to see you try this on, Em. The color is gonna look great on you."

"I repeat, where's the rest of it?" Emma grinned, playful.

The sales ladies had arrived next to their little group. "Can I setup a fitting room for you? I'd be happy to take these to hang in the dressing room."

Emma pulled at Jaxson's arm to pull him closer. "I really do need to em... well... you know. Can't we go home and come back tomorrow?"

"Don't be ridiculous. You just need to go to the bathroom and then come back." Before she could protest, he turned to the sales lady to ask, "Where is the nearest ladies room? You wouldn't have one here in the store by chance, would you?"

The women exchanged conspiratorial glances. "Well technically no. There is just a small one in the back for employees. We are only supposed to let customers use it in the case of emergencies."

Chase threw the women a flirty smile. "Well this is an emergency of sorts." He glanced at Emma and she panicked. Surely he wouldn't go there.

"Emma here has been naughty. She needs some privacy to... well... let's just say she has to remove her punishment."

The women's mouths opened wide in shock over what Chase had just said. No one was more surprised than Emma though. How dare he talk about their private relationship to total strangers? She was just about to let him have it when Jaxson linked his hand in hers and led her towards the back of the store. She tried to pull him to a stop, but he was too strong.

"Please, Jaxson. I want to go home. Don't make me do this here."

"You're being punished, Emma. The purpose of a punishment is not to make it as easy as I can. It's to make you never want to repeat your mistake again. If you don't like being treated like a naughty girl, then I suggest you refrain from putting yourself down in the future."

She wanted the floor to open up and swallow her then and there. They waited for one of the sales girls to escort them to the back of the store, using a key on a ring to open the door to a small bathroom. She rushed into the room, happy to get away from the smirking grin on the petite sales lady's face. She rushed to close the door, almost slamming it in Jaxson's face. He and Chase both pressed into the small room with her and slammed the door closed.

"Oh no. You guys are not staying in here with me. No way. No how."

"You're no fun," Chase teased.

Jaxson made her wait for his answer, but he finally folded. "Fine, we'll leave, but not until after we take the plug out for you. After you're done I want you to wash it and then knock on the door. We'll come back to push it back in."

"But... I thought it was over now."

"Nope. Not until bedtime tonight."

She tried to think logically. "There's no way you'll get it back in without lube. We'll have to wait..."

She was cut off by Jaxson pulling a small tube of lube out of his pocket with a grin. "I picked up an extra travel size when we were at the store earlier. I figured I should start carrying. You never know when the mood may strike. Aren't I a good boy scout?"

"Just brilliant," she replied dripping sarcasm.

He didn't seem upset in the least. "Turn around, sweetheart. Lean over and put your hands on the sink."

Emma moved slowly, following directions. Chase stepped behind her, reaching around to unsnap her capri pants, lowering her zipper and pressing her pants to fall around her ankles.

"Bend over farther for me, honey. Stick that beautiful ass out for me."

Emma closed her eyes to avoid seeing her flaming face in the mirror above the sink. She thrust her ass out, knowing her men were admiring the look of the anal plug jutting out of her bottom.

"The bruising isn't too bad today. Be glad I stopped at ten or you'd be sporting some significant bruises on this bootie of yours."

He'd been twirling the plug as he spoke. She both hated and loved what he was doing to her. More accurately, she wanted to hate what he was doing, but she couldn't. It felt too fantastic. The fullness. His dominance. The tenderness painting her ass. It all added up to an overwhelming desire to surrender. She wouldn't tell the men, but they could ask her anything in that moment and she'd do it.

She felt bereft without the fullness as soon as the hardness left her body in a quick rush. Jaxson reached around her to throw the toy into the sink.

The hard slap to her bare globe got her attention, snapping her eyes up to look at the men standing behind her through the reflection of the mirror. She saw their desire shining back at her. They wanted her.

"Five minutes, Emma. We'll be back and will help you get put back together."

The five minutes flew by, but she was ready for them when they returned, knocking softly before entering. She was just drying the hard toy. Her bottom hole was sore and she wasn't looking forward to it being filled again, but she knew better than to ask for a reprieve.

She handed the plug to Jaxson reluctantly.

"Chase, sit on the toilet. Emma, stand in front of him and lean over so he's holding onto your torso."

They moved to follow directions and within seconds, Emma had her ass thrust out towards her Dom as he used his feet to move her legs to a wider stance. Emma tried to look down into Chase's lap, but he wouldn't allow it. He lifted her chin from her chest to look up into his beautiful, brown eyes.

"Keep your eyes open and on me, honey."

The drizzle of lube was cold against her overheated body. Like the night before, Jaxson took a couple of minutes to swish the lube generously around her pucker, inserting two fingers to loosen her. The hard tip of the plug pressed against her tender rosette. It didn't take much effort to seat it this time. Her body welcomed it back inside as if it belonged there.

She was about to stand when she felt Jaxson's fingers exploring lower, sliding through her slick crease. It felt amazing. If it weren't for the suspicion there were two sales ladies eavesdropping on the other side of the thin door, she'd beg him to fuck her here and now. She'd been on edge all day.

Chase leaned in to kiss her tenderly, their tongues exploring just as Jaxson's fingers explored below. His slight pinch to her clit sent jolts of desire through her, setting her to rocking her ass back and forth in an attempt to bring more friction to her neglected body part

She was so close to coming. Her brain knew she shouldn't. Not without permission, especially after a punishment, but she wanted it bad. Needed it even.

His fingers were gone in an instant, used to slap her ass several times while she groaned her disappointment.

Jaxson chuckled behind her as he leaned down to pull her pants and panties up as Chase grinned in front of her.

"That was not nice," she pouted.

"You can wait a few more hours." Jaxson hugged her sliding his hand over the hard plug, pressing it deeper.

"Yes, sir." The dominance in his eyes melted her insides into a pool of goo. God she wanted him bad.

After washing up, Emma let her men lead her out of the small room where sure enough, the two sales ladies were waiting for them. She wondered who was taking care of other customers if they were back here spying on the threesome.

"Mr. Davidson, we've setup a fitting room for you if you'd like to follow me sir."

So they knew who the men were. Of course they did. Everyone did.

The men took a seat in the chairs near the three-way mirror. Emma spent the next thirty minutes trying on skimpy clothes and modeling them for her model boyfriends. She tried not to be self-conscious of her soft tummy and rounded bottom as they filled out the racy undergarments in a way very unlike the hundreds of thin models the men worked with every day. If the hard erections filling out their jeans were any indication, they really were telling the truth when they told her how sexy her curves were.

They ended up spending a small fortune to outfit her with an entirely new intimate wardrobe, but considering the best thing she had at home was a lacy black bra and panty set from Kohl's, she considered it money well spent.

They were halfway through dinner at Emma's favorite Italian restaurant when her phone lit up with several incoming texts.

She dug her phone out of her purse to find a series of text messages and pictures from Courtney.

"Shit."

"What is it, sweetheart?"

"One day. We left the house for one day."

"And it was a good day." Chase grinned, his mouth full of pasta.

"I'm not sure you'll still say that when you see this."

She handed her phone over so the men who were sitting on the other side of the booth could scroll through the texts.

"Well fuck. This might complicate things a bit."

"You think?" Emma tried to stay calm.

The pictures showed two news vans parked outside her off-campus house. They had crews mulling around as if they were ready to pounce the second the threesome drove up.

"I'm guessing it was the rude chick in the grocery store," Chase observed.

Jaxson countered, "My bets on the quiet one taking pictures."

The men bantered back and forth as they chowed down.

"Hello? Why aren't you guys more upset by this?"

Jaxson pinned her with a serious look. "I think the real question here is why are *you*? What's the big deal?"

"Easy for you to say. You're used to being recognized everywhere."

She didn't like the silence that fell over the table. Or the probing stare flashed her way.

Chase asked quietly, "Tell us, Em. What's got you spooked?"

They'd gone full circle from their blow up in the middle of the night. She worked hard to find the right words to answer their question. Looking for words that wouldn't result in getting her ass lit up with the paddle again when they got home.

"I'm just not used to the attention, you know? You've been in the spotlight so long I think you forgot what it's like to be anonymous. I'm not looking forward to reporters digging into my past and interviewing my friends and family. I feel bad that I've brought this attention onto my housemates. Now they're holed up in the house so they don't have to walk the gauntlet of reporters."

"I'm sorry this is going to effect them, but we'll be leaving soon so it won't be for long."

Chase raised his hand to flag the server down for their check. As much as she wanted to put it off, she knew they'd eventually have to brave the press. In fact, the line of fans started in the lobby of the restaurant before they could even make it to their truck. Several families stopped them as they pressed towards the door, begging for an autograph or pictures with the celebrities. The models were gracious, scribbling their signatures on the scraps of paper shoved towards them and posing for photos with the handful of well-wishers.

It was only once they were all three safely in the cab of their truck heading away from the restaurant that the awkward silence filled the space.

Emma had to ask. "So, is that what it's like everywhere you go? People surrounding you. Touching you. Asking for pictures or autographs?" She tried not to let her voice sound as afraid as she felt at the thought of that happening everywhere they went.

Chase tried to make light of it. "It's not so bad most of the time. If we know there will be a crush of fans, we usually have security guards with us or sometimes we wear disguises so we can't be recognized."

"Just great. I've always hated Halloween."

Jaxson reached for her hand. "It'll just take you some time to get used to it, baby. We won't let anything happen to you."

She knew they'd keep her physically safe. She couldn't tell him that it was her emotional state she was most worried about. She would only be able to take so much negative press pointing out the men were crazy to be sharing one plump grad student when they could literally pick any woman they wanted in the entire world.

She'd been zoning out, not paying attention so Jaxson's question caught her off-guard. "How does that sound?"

"Sorry. I wasn't paying attention."

"I asked if you'd feel better heading to a hotel instead of your house for the rest of the time we're in town. We had a suite reserved but then I called to cancel."

It was tempting. The idea of having to pass through lines of paparazzi to get to her own off-campus house was ludicrous, yet she couldn't very well get her things packed up and moved back to her parents from afar.

"Naw. We have to face it eventually. Might as well be tonight."

They were only a few minutes away from her house as they drove in silence. Emma sat in the middle of the bench seat, wringing her hands in her lap nervously. She reached out to flick on the radio, hoping to fill the quiet with calming music. The sound of a hard rock song banging out a funky rhythm filled the space.

She'd never heard the song and got caught up in the heavy beat, allowing it to wash over her, helping to forget what awaited her at her home.

The song was just wrapping as they turned down her street. The announcer let her know it had been the newest release by the red-hot Crushing Stones band. They would be playing in nearby Milwaukee in two weeks.

"I thought that sounded like Cash and the guys." Chase piped in.

Jaxson grinned. "We should call and give him shit for not getting us his newest material ahead of the public."

Emma just shook her head. "You know the hottest band in the country?"

Chase teased her, "Why, you looking to ditch us for someone new already?"

"Oh yeah, as if Cash Carter would be my type. He changes women more often than he changes his clothes."

Her men just grinned. "That might be true, but we know lots of hot bands... and singers... athletes... actors... politicians. Anyone special you'd like to meet? We can make it happen." Jaxson assured her as if it were the most normal thing in the world to know famous people.

"Oh I don't know. I guess I wouldn't mind meeting the Queen of England." She purposefully suggested the impossible to make her point.

"Sounds good. We'll be in London next week, although I'd suggest you meet the younger generation. They're much less stuffy."

They slowed the truck as they approached the house to avoid running over the pressing media surrounding their truck. Flashes of cameras lit up the darkening sky.

"You ready?" Jaxson had pulled her hand into his, squeezing her gently in contrast to the pounding against the windows as the media grew impatient.

The men grabbed their many bags from shopping and counted down backwards from three – two – one... and they were off, pressing through the crowd, not stopping to answer questions. Not stopping to pose for photos. Just quietly pushing through the throng until they arrived at the front door.

The door flew open from the inside, held open by Ryan who slammed it closed as soon as they were inside.

All her roommates greeted them in the front room. They all stood still, unsure what the right thing to say was in a situation such as this.

Ryan gave it a shot. "So, this is fun. You think we can charge a fee for parking on our front lawn? Maybe we could all pay down our student loans."

Emma opened her mouth to apologize to her roommates, but Jaxson shushed her.

"Chase and I are sorry you are all getting caught up in this, but we really do appreciate the privacy you've given the three of us the last few weeks. I know you could have gone to the press a long time ago and you didn't. We will be helping Emma pack up tonight and tomorrow morning and taking her stuff to her parents. Then we can stay at the hotel next to campus until we leave town so we don't bother you."

Courtney looked shocked. "Wait. Why are you packing up Emma's stuff too?" She pinned Emma with a wide-eyes stare.

She wished Jaxson would do the talking for her again, but he didn't. He did slip his arm around her waist as of to fortify her courage to say the words she was still struggling with.

"Well... see... I'm going to go on the road with Jax and Chase for a while. I'll try to finish my grad school attending remote classes."

"You bitch. I'm so jealous of you!"

"Court, that's enough!" Her boyfriend Ryan popped her bottom a couple of times to make his point.

Richard looked downright green with envy. "You are the luckiest girl in the world, Emma. I hope you know that."

"Oh I do, Richard. Believe me, I know how lucky I am."

CHAPTER 18

*J*axson pulled up to the closed gate of his parent's spacious estate located not far from Mount Vernon, Virginia. He pressed the button on the security stand to announce his arrival and looked into the camera trained on him. Within seconds the wrought-iron gate started to open.

They'd been expecting him.

The historical mansion was set back from the private road. A winding driveway led the way to the two-story colonial. Summer flowers were in bloom everywhere he looked giving the manicured grounds the air of a royal property. He had to hand it to Juan, his parent's long time gardener. He sure had a talent for landscaping.

He pulled his Audi into a parking spot to the right of the main house. He had just stepped out of the car when his mom came hustling down the front steps, a mega-watt smile on her face.

A pang of guilt hit Jaxson. His father may not deserve his love or loyalty, but his mom had done her best to shield her only son from the political fallout that came with having a public figure for a father.

"Jaxson!" She flew into his arms, hugging him with the

unbound love of a mother. It was in that moment he pledged to do a better job of staying in touch with the woman in his arms.

He chuckled as she squeezed him harder. "I missed you too, Mom."

The attractive woman in her fifties leaned back to take a good look at her son. Jax took the opportunity to do the same and he didn't like what he found.

Despite her many surgeries meant to lock in her youthful beauty, she was showing signs of her age in a way he'd never noticed before.

"You look more handsome than ever." His mom moved her right palm up to cup his scruff-covered face. A genuine smile lit up her face. "You look more relaxed. Happy even."

"You say that like I've never been happy."

She got serious. "Have you been? I mean really happy?"

Her question took him by surprise. They normally followed an unspoken agreement not to ask any questions that might lead to a disagreement. It took him a second to formulate a truthful response. "I wasn't unhappy."

A sad smile played at her lips. "Spoken like your father's son. The apple didn't fall far from the tree."

They so rarely talked about the wedge between them—his father. He wasn't sure he wanted to go there now either, but she was right about one thing.

He was happy. Really happy. Maybe for the first time in his adult life. Being in love changed everything. Apparently even his relationship with his mother.

He asked her his own version of personal question. "Why do you stay, mom?"

Emotions flitted across her face until her politician's wife mask was firmly affixed. He knew before she spoke he'd pushed too hard too fast.

"Don't ask silly questions. I love your father."

They both knew that was a lie, but like the past, he let it go.

He'd tried many times to get her to leave. He may never know the real reason she stayed, but he knew he would not be the one to change her mind.

His mom linked her arm through his and pulled him towards the house. "Come inside. Cook prepared all of your favorites for you. I'd kinda hoped you'd bring that new girlfriend of yours. I'm guessing she's what's making you happy."

He should have known the local news in Madison might leak national. "She is making me happy, but it's complicated."

"Isn't everything in life?"

They'd made it to the front door. A gust of cool air hit them as a butler Jaxson had never seen before opened the door for them. It was over eighty degrees outside so the A/C felt great.

"Welcome home, Mr. Davidson."

"Thanks, but this isn't home. I'm just visiting."

He didn't miss the pained look on his mother's face before her mask returned. He supposed he could have let the comment slide to make her happy, but he didn't want there to be any misunderstanding. He would never live under the same roof as his father again. And this building would never be home.

His parents had moved there when he'd left for college so it had never felt like home. Instead, he always felt like he was on a tour of a museum when he visited. That or the stage of a movie set.

Everything was immaculate. Tasteful artwork adorned every nook and cranny, most chosen not for sentimental value or even because of his parent's tastes, but to maximize their illusion of wealth and power. There were no personal knick-knacks from vacations past. No family photos from the beach or school field trips. The only photos of their son were framed magazine covers meant to impress.

No. His parents surrounded themselves with worldly gifts from foreign leaders. Artifacts meant to distract visitors from noticing everything was an illusion.

Jaxson tried to change the subject as they walked to the dining room. "The grounds look magnificent. Juan sure has everything blooming beautifully."

He caught the panic in his mother's face just as they entered the dining room. His father was seated at the head of the table, talking on his cell phone while watching something on the laptop in front of him. His only acknowledgment of Jaxson was a small nod in his direction.

His mother leaned in to whisper, "Don't talk about Juan with your father."

Jaxson turned to see his mother's blush. He had no idea what that was about, but was curious.

"Jaxson. Welcome home." His father had finally ended his call, but didn't bother to stand to greet his son.

"Thanks, but it's just a visit."

Unlike his mother, his comment had no effect on his father. "Of course. Of course. You're off living your life in parts unknown. I'm just lucky you had some time off for a short visit. This is a big week for me."

Typical. It's always about him.

"Yeah, I've been on vacation for a few weeks, but I'm headed back to Europe soon."

They'd taken their seats at the end of the long dining table. His father at the end, as always, while Jax sat across from his mother.

The second their asses hit the chairs, two serving girls in pressed grey uniform dresses came in with the first course. Only his parents would have a formal luncheon for three on a Thursday noon. And for their son, no less. He wasn't sure why it pissed him off, but it did. It was in direct conflict of the real life he'd been enjoying with his lovers. Eating breakfast cereal or cold pizza and watching old reruns. Playing board games, video games and laughing.

Not much laughing went on in this house. It made him sad for his mother.

An awkward silence had fallen over the threesome. Jaxson tried to come up with a topic—anything—that wouldn't incite an argument with his father. Since they disagreed on almost everything, it didn't leave many subjects available.

"So have you been doing much traveling?"

Instead of answering, his father stopped the soupspoon half way to his mouth to stare. "Don't you watch the news?"

Jaxson hated to tell him, but he actually avoided watching the news as much as possible just to stay away from stories about his father that would piss him off.

"I'm afraid you'll have to fill me in. I've been pretty busy."

"I'm running for a national office. I travel every single day."

"Yeah, well I guess I meant for fun. You know... vacation... golfing... swimming... maybe sleeping in?"

"I don't have time for goofing off. There's too much to do." The elder man's voice dripped with distain at the thought of doing anything fun. Jaxson felt another pang of regret for his mother.

Strike one.

Several more minutes of awkward silence went by before Jaxson tried again. "I saw a lot of changes happening down in Georgetown. Looks like a lot of new development just off campus."

Progress. His father didn't respond with impatience or anger. In fact, he didn't respond at all.

Strike two.

The uneasy silence as the servers cleared the soup dishes and slid plates of salad in front of the three occupants of the room started to piss Jaxson off. Communicating with the people who'd brought him into the world shouldn't be this hard.

Not for the first time, he thought about how lucky he was to even be alive because if there were ever two people who should have never had children, it was his parents. They sucked at it.

He speared a small tomato and popped it in his mouth, deciding on his next topic. He went for broke.

"The estate looks beautiful. Juan sure is doing a great job with the flowers. How is he doing anyway? He have any more grandchildren?"

The clatter of his mother's silverware against her salad plate broke the steely silence. Jaxson glanced her way to see the blood draining from her face. Her mask was gone—replaced by fear.

He swung his gaze towards his father. It appeared all of the blood from his mother had rushed into his father's face. Angry didn't even begin to describe the look on the senator.

"We do not mention that name in this house."

Jaxson was truly bewildered. Juan, and his family, was the closest thing he'd had to an extended family growing up. Jaxson had played with Juan's kids and even helped with the gardening until his father had found out and forbid him to help again stating it was beneath him.

"I don't understand. Did Juan do something wrong?"

His father put down the fork he'd been holding, placed his elbows on the armrests of the formal dining chair and steepled his fingers as he pinned his son with a dominant glare.

"He falsified his documents when he applied to work for me. He was not a legal citizen and should not have been employed. His lying has given my opponents fodder to attack me with."

"What the hell are you talking about? We've always known he came over from Mexico. He's been sending money back to his mother and sister forever."

"Just because I knew he was of Mexican descent does not mean I knew he wasn't a legal resident."

He saw the quiver of his mother's lips as she whispered a warning to let the subject drop. Her head moved slightly from side to side.

Well fuck that.

"What a crock of bullshit. You knew all along. You paid him cash under the table for years because it saved you a few bucks. Don't blame that on Juan."

If there were a thermometer in the room, it would show the temperature falling like a rock as the two men stared at each other. There was a time in his life Jaxson would have backed down, afraid of his father. That time had past.

His father covered his tracks. "Well, that's not how I remember it. And it's not how your mother remembers it either. In fact, she's sworn under oath so I'd be very careful with your accusations. I'd sure hate to see your mother in legal trouble because you shot your mouth off to the wrong person with lies."

"So what? You just threw Juan and his family to the wolves? Blaming him?"

"Damn right I did. He did something illegal. I had him deported."

Jaxson was on his feet. "You did what?"

"Sit down. You're acting like a brash child."

"No, father. I'm acting like a person who cares about someone who was nice to me as a kid. Like a person who isn't afraid to call bullshit when he sees it."

"Juan and his family made plenty of money with me over the years. If he invested wisely, he's going to be fine."

"And if he didn't? He spent twenty years working for you and this is how you repay him? You make me sick."

"You disappoint me yet again, Jaxson. You are still the idealist, trying to see the world through rose-colored glasses. Surely you can see that when you reach my level of power, difficult decisions must be made. You need to toughen up, or you'll continue to get run over in life."

"Toughen up? Is that all you have to say about throwing the closest thing I'll ever have to an uncle or family friend to the wolves? Toughen up?"

"I see you are still using your Bachelor of Arts degree with your melodramatic outbursts."

Jaxson pushed his chair back and started for the door. He

never should have come here. His father was only getting worse with time. Power was corrupting him.

He was almost to the door when his father called out to him. "We had a deal. You promised. I've sunk a lot of money into advertising your presence tomorrow night when I make my official announcement. I wouldn't back out on your promise if I were you."

Jaxson swung back to face off with the elder man who sat at the head of the table, cool as the cucumber he had just put into his mouth.

The silence dragged on until Jaxson pressed him. "Tell me, Dad... are you still voting against anything that might help low and middle income families?"

"If you are asking if I still oppose giving handouts out to people who refuse to carry their weight in society, the answer is yes."

"I see. Bet your still enjoying excellent health care while millions of Americans can't even afford to buy vital medication or get treatment for their loved ones."

"Oh please. Cry me a river why don't you?"

"I see. And how about immigration reform? Environmental causes? Education reform? Have you changed your stance on anything since we last debated?"

"I do not flip-flop. I am on the record on all of those topics."

"Oh yes, I bet you are. How about your support for the LGBT community?"

"Don't ask stupid questions, Jaxson. There's no room in this country for sinners who choose to flaunt their queer lifestyles. Now, why on earth are you grilling me as if we were in a debate?"

"Oh I don't know, *Dad*. Maybe because I'm still trying to figure out who I should vote for next year."

That got a spark of agitation from the senator.

"Come sit back down. I'd like to hear more about this girl-friend your mother tells me about."

Jaxson shot his mother daggers. The whole reason he'd come solo today and planned on attending the gala the next night alone was to shield Emma from all of this kind of bullshit. Chase had met his parents enough to know to steer clear.

"You leave Emma out of this. She has nothing to do with this discussion."

"Of course she does. My campaign manager tells me that you settling down with an All-American girl like her would be good for our family image. Of course she needs to come tomorrow night."

Jaxson answered with a belly-roll laugh. "That's a good one. You actually think I'd subject her to the toxic people of DC?" Then it dawned on him to ask. "And what would you know about her anyway?"

His father finished leisurely chewing his bite of salad before answering with force. "I had the FBI run a background check on her and her family, of course."

He didn't know how he got to his father's chair so fast. His body just flew at him in a hazy rage. "How dare you! You so much as say her name in the future and I'll ruin you."

"Relax. You are too stressed out, Jax."

"Say it. You're going to stay away from Emma."

"I'm afraid it's too late for that. I sent Bonnie over to your loft this morning. If I'm not mistaken, they've already hit several boutiques. Bonnie has my gold card. Money is no object. I want her to look her best. Too bad we don't have a few more weeks to have her take a few pounds off."

Jaxson's fist connected with his father's jaw so hard the older man's chair tipped sideways, crashing to the floor and depositing his father onto the priceless Ming dynasty carpet.

"You are a piece of shit, you know that? You may have the rest of the world fooled, but I know the truth. You stay away from Emma. You stay away from Chase. You stay away from me. Got it?"

Several security guards rushed into the room. One went to assist his father up, and the second stepped between the two men, pressing Jaxson back by pushing his chest.

He could hear his mother crying behind him. He hated that he'd upset her, but in the end, her refusal to leave her father would forever hold her hostage to his bullshit.

He was about to turn again to leave when his father was on his feet, approaching him as he rubbed his jaw. Raw fury shone in the elder's eyes as he pressed the security guard aside to stand nose to nose with his son. They were the same height and build, but Jaxson's youth would always give him the edge in a fistfight.

Instead of pounding his son with his fists, his father hit him with threats instead.

"Don't think for one minute that I can't bring your modeling career to a screeching halt. A few phone calls and your life of leisure goes up in smoke, and don't forget it. I am Gregory David-son." Jaxson always wanted to laugh when his father would announce his name, as if his son might forget it. "Now, this is how it's gonna go. You and your girlfriend are going to follow through on the promise you made me and then you can gallivant off into the sunset. Just stay out of the limelight and don't do anything that would bring negative publicity to my campaign and I couldn't care less if you sit around eating pizzas and fucking like rabbits twenty-four seven."

"You are some piece of work, you know that?" It was in that moment of clarity that Jaxson knew exactly what he needed to do. "Fine, I'll keep my promise. In fact, I'll even bring Emma to the gala for the photo op, but then I'm out of here."

"Fine by me."

The men squared off for several long seconds before Jaxson announced, "It was nice to see you, mother. My compliments to Cook. Let her know I'm sorry I couldn't stay for the next course, but I suddenly lost my appetite. I'll see you tomorrow night."

Jaxson didn't stop until he was seated behind the wheel where he took several cleansing breaths, trying to steady his pulse after the run-in with his father. He was shaking with pent up emotion.

He couldn't wait to get back to the loft and his lovers and best friends. His only shot at normalcy was with Chase and Emma. He hated putting them in danger, but he couldn't sit by idle while his father tried to bamboozle the entire nation.

CHAPTER 19

"*J* can't believe how much money you spent today, Chase. Isn't Jaxson going to be angry?"

Emma and Chase's arms were so full they'd had to tip the doorman to accompany them in the elevator to Jaxson's George-town loft just to get all of their purchases upstairs.

"Trust me, he won't be mad at all. He wanted me to help pick out some fun new clothes for you for our trip."

"Clothes I get. But you bought shoes, purses, scarves, jewelry... hell even luggage."

"Hey, it's all about the accessories, sweetheart."

Emma caught her reflection in the mirrored elevator door and almost didn't recognize herself. New haircut and highlights... mani... pedi... designer clothes. She was a new woman.

The elevator dinged their arrival at the top floor of the four-teen-story building. Jaxson had purchased the penthouse loft four years earlier and then remodeled it to the top-of-the-line everything.

It was a long walk to the end of the hall. They'd been gone all day and Emma's feet were killing her. She'd worn new high-heeled sandals that proved to be fashionable, yet painful.

Chase stepped in front of her to wrangle with the lock as he reminded her, "Don't forget, Jaxson's father paid for almost half of this stuff anyway."

Oh she hadn't forgotten. The arrival of Bonnie, the senator's personal assistant, had confused her greatly. If Emma weren't going with Jaxson to the gala event the next night, why would she need a grand ball gown? She'd tried to discuss it with Chase, but he'd gone all Dom on her and told her to be a good girl and just let them take care of her.

They dumped their packages just inside the door on the foyer's Italian marble floor. Chase tipped the doorman for his help and showed him out before the two of them left the entrance, planning on collapsing into the plush leather couches of the open great room.

Chase pulled them to a quick stop just inside the room. They hadn't expected Jaxson home for several hours, yet there he was, his back to them as he stood looking out the two-story wall of windows down onto the Georgetown University campus and surrounding neighborhood below them. He had to have heard them arrive, yet he maintained his perch.

Something was wrong.

She could hear the strain in Chase's voice as he questioned Jax. "This is a surprise. We didn't expect to see you home so early."

It took Jax several long seconds to turn to greet them. His dark eyes looked stormy. The rock glass half-filled with an amber liquid shook in his hand as if he might drop it any second.

Emma rushed forward, not stopping until she hugged him as hard as possible. Her choke-hold managed to free a chuckle from her Dom. "I missed you too, honey. Did you have fun today?"

She could feel his arms closing around her as he hugged her back. His lean muscles were tense under his three-piece suit. She ran her hands up and down his back, trying to massage the stress out of him through the expensive fabric. The feel of Chase closing in behind her, turning her into the middle of their sandwich as he hugged them both helped Jaxson relax further. The threesome held steady, silently enjoying their innocent intimacy.

"What an awesome hello. I needed this." Jaxson's voice sounded calmer already. "Did you two have fun today?"

Chase answered for them. "Did you know Bonnie was coming over to take us shopping for the gala?"

The men each stepped back, ruining their sandwich and leaving her feeling vulnerable and alone. Sensing her loose end, Jaxson pulled her to the nearby seating arrangement and sat, pulling her into his lap before answering.

"Yeah, the old man was kind enough to inform me what he'd done after it was too late."

Chase plopped down across from them answering, "I wish I could have seen his face when you told him to fuck off—that we weren't coming."

Emma had tucked her head into the crook of Jaxson's neck, unable to see his face, but his silence in light of the question hanging in the air spoke volumes.

Chase pressed him. "You did tell him, right?"

"Of course I told him, but... well shit, you know him. He doesn't take no well."

"That's tough shit. I don't care about myself, but we can't put Emma in that position." Chase persisted.

"I agree, but..." Jaxson was hedging.

"No but. Going is not an option."

Emma tucked in closer, not wanting to hear the rising tension between her lovers.

Jaxson countered, "He fired Juan. Fucking deported him and his entire family."

"Holy shit. I'm so sorry."

Emma had no clue who Juan was, but it sounded as if Chase were paying his condolences for losing a loved one. That confused her.

Jaxson's voice was raising, he was as angry as she'd ever seen him. "He's as nasty as ever. Totally obnoxious on every issue we care about. Hell, we even threw punches before I got escorted out by security."

"Then that's all the more reason," Chase insisted.

"You're right. I just thought... never mind. It was a crazy idea."

Emma wiggled in his lap until she could see Jaxson's face. She needed to understand what was happening. Why he sounded so uncertain. It was so unlike him. "What is it? What aren't you saying?"

"It's nothing, baby. You look tired. Why don't you go in and lay down for a short nap. I need to take Chase out and show him an investment property I'm thinking of buying. We'll wake you up when we get back and are ready for some dinner and a little play time."

He wasn't asking her. He was back to his Dom voice. He wasn't ready to discuss what had happened with his father yet. It hurt to know he couldn't trust her enough to let her know what was going on.

She pushed to her feet and before she could say something that might end up with her over someone's lap, she stomped off to the bedroom with a sassy, "fine," as her only response.

* * *

JUST OVER TWENTY-FOUR HOURS LATER, Emma was looking at her reflection in the three-way mirror in the oversized bathroom of Jaxson's loft. The day had been a whirlwind of preparations, not only for their upcoming extended trip to London, but unbelievably she was being primped to attend Jaxson's father's fundraiser where he would be announcing his official candidacy for the president of the United States of America.

That she would even be in attendance was incredible enough. That the current plan was for her to be on the stage standing beside the candidate's son as the announcement was made was truly insane.

She tried to sit sill as the make-up artist and hairdresser her men had hired to assist fawned all over her. The rented diamond necklace and teardrop earrings sparkled in the bright lights reminding her she wasn't in Kansas anymore.

The last day had taken on a fantasy quality as she'd been coached and prepped on proper etiquette for hobnobbing with the rich and famous. Jaxson had told her at least ten times that he honestly couldn't care less about what anyone thought, yet he knew she was desperate not to do anything that might draw negative attention to herself.

When the stylist finished and stepped away so she could get a good look at her reflection, Emma almost accused them of replacing the mirror with a life-sized picture of a princess. Her long, thick hair was atop her head in a magnificent up-do. Her eyes took on a smoky, mystical quality that only made her unique lavender eyes stand out even more. As she glanced lower, she loved the cut of her dress that accentuated her ample breasts tastefully while cinching in her waist to make her look thinner. It didn't hurt that she'd barely eaten for the last two days, both nervous and hopeful to shed a few pounds before stepping into the public eye with the men again.

"Holy hotness. Emma, you look good enough to eat." Chase and Jaxson stood just inside the room, looking every inch the GC models they were in their black Armani tuxedos. Her eyes met their heated gaze in the mirror. She'd seen that feral look of desire many times before. Her body was conditioned to respond and right on cue, she felt a wet gush release into her new lace panties as her men moved closer, looking like predators ready to pounce.

"Hello," she said simply.

"Well, hello little lady. I think we should all stay home tonight." It was Chase teasing, yet the comment hit close to home.

Jaxson replied, "Hey, I told you guys you can stay home. You don't need to go tonight. I can handle this on my own," he rationalized.

"Like hell you can. After hearing all the shit your father has planned, there's no way in hell you're going into the lion's den without your support crew." Chase didn't back down, smiling at Emma supportively.

She was grateful her lovers had sat her down the night before. They'd spent hours talking through the pros and cons of going as a group to the gala that evening. Her heart swelled with love for the men as she remembered how they'd left the final decision entirely up to her, recognizing she had the most emotional vulnerability wrapped up in how they went public with their relationship.

Emma didn't like how defenseless her Dom looked in that moment. She was grateful that Chase seemed to step in, as if he knew Jaxson needed him to take the lead. Chase reminded them of their motto they'd adopted less than twenty-four hours before. "Where you go, we all go."

Jaxson held out his bent arm, waiting for Emma to place her hand through the crook. Chase closed in on her other side, placing his arm around her waist. They made their way to the elevator linked, stepping in and all taking a deep breath, knowing this would be their last moment of peace for many hours.

The lobby of their building was quiet, yet the row of news vans and paparazzi with their zoom-lens cameras trained on the glass door was already lined up outside, ready to greet them.

Oh how she wished they could leave through a back door or something— anything to avoid having to see pictures of herself plastered on the front of gossip magazines with headlines like "Jaxson Davidson Dating Unnamed Grad Student." She'd especially enjoyed being described by the Chicago Tribune as his 'chunky co-ed.'

The door was too narrow to retain their three-wide stride.

Chase leaned in to kiss her cheek before dropping back to follow as Jaxson led her to the wolves.

The click of cameras shuttering greeted them just before reporters shouted out questions, hoping they might stop for an impromptu interview. She plastered on a smile as they moved towards the waiting stretch limousine in slow motion, unable to cut through the pressing crowd quickly. Emma dreaded arriving at the gala if this was how insane the coverage was at Jaxson's home.

Chase pressed in close to make sure no one could ambush her and Jaxson from behind. Men in suits with earpieces stepped up from the limousine to escort them the final steps through the crowd. Still, in spite of all of the men surrounding her to keep her safe, Emma felt more than one hand groping at her, daring to touch her. She fought down the panic.

Only once they were safely ensconced in the back of the limo along with the two armed-guards she suspected might be secret service agents did she take a calming breath.

"Well, that was fun. I can't believe you guys live like this."

Chase grabbed her hand. "This was worse than normal. It won't be like this when we get out of DC. At least I hope not."

Jaxson was on her other side. She suspected he didn't realize he was squeezing her hand so hard it was starting to hurt. He'd been unusually quiet the last twenty-four hours since they'd all debated back and forth the pros and cons of them all attending the gala tonight. Truth be told, Emma wouldn't be surprised if he changed his mind yet again before they exited the limousine, and sent his lovers back to the loft to wait for him.

The summer evening was warm, drawing out tourists and residents alike. The driver took them past the White House on their way across town to the Grand Hyatt Washington DC. With each block they drove, Emma's dread grew. The words were on the tip of her tongue. She didn't really want to do this. Had she made the right decision when she and Chase had insisted on attending to support Jaxson?

Jaxson picked up on her hesitation. "It's not too late, you know. I can send you two back to the loft. I'll just stay until after the announcement and then be done with it."

He wasn't talking to Chase. He was talking to her. Giving her the option to hightail it out of danger.

Oh how she wanted to leave, but as she glanced back and forth between her handsome lovers, her heart expanded with love. She loved them with all her heart. She'd known when she agreed to follow them as they'd left Wisconsin that there would be days like this. Days where she'd feel inadequate. Out of her element. She'd promised herself she wouldn't hide away, too afraid to be seen for fear of negative gossip.

Four hands massaged her, gently knocking out the kinks brought on by tension. Emma closed her eyes, enjoying the feeling of being taken care of by her lovers.

When the car stopped, she knew she was out of time. She opened her eyes to look between her men, greeting them with a smile.

"Where you go, we all go," she replied.

She'd made the right decision when she recognized the relief on her Dom's face. "Yes, ma'am," Jaxson teased back.

The driver had come to open the door nearest their seat. They let one secret service guard out first, followed by Chase. They could make out clapping by the crowd surrounding the red carpet lining the path from the carport to the grand lobby. Jaxson kissed her nose, careful not to mess up her lipstick and then stepped out next.

The men spent a minute waving and posing for the paparazzi like the celebrities they were. Only after the hubbub died down did Jaxson lean back in the car, offering her his outstretched hand like an olive branch. Emma grabbed on, hanging on for dear life as she allowed herself to be pulled from the safety of the car. The last guard brought up the rear as their small entourage made their way through the clicking cameras and press of fans trying to get photos and autographs.

Emma went through the motions, floating through the scene like an outside observer, watching the spectacle as a bystander instead of the co-star of Jaxson's life. It was the only way she got through the crowd without feeling claustrophobic.

Things got marginally better once they were in the lobby of the upscale hotel. Bonnie met them as they crossed the space.

"Thank you for coming, Jaxson. Your father was very pleased to hear you and Emma had arrived." She glanced nervously at Chase standing next to Emma. "I didn't inform him that Chase had come against his express wishes. I thought I made that clear yesterday when we were shopping. I hope he doesn't decide to make it an issue."

Jaxson tensed, ready to fight to keep them together, but Chase disarmed the problem, flashing his signature smile that brought out his dimples. "No offense taken, Bonnie. And here I thought I was your favorite."

The professional woman in her forties actually blushed like a schoolgirl, "Don't be such a flirt. You know I love having you around, but I do work for Senator Davidson and so what he wants, he gets."

Jaxson groused, "That's why we're here. Mind if we get out of the main thoroughfare here?"

Bonnie and the security guards escorted them past the line of political supporters who had undoubtedly paid an exorbitant amount per plate for the privilege of attending the grand event. The irony was not lost on Emma that she'd have paid just as much to stay at the loft.

Just inside the ballroom, Jaxson's parents stood to the side in a receiving line of sorts, greeting guests as they arrived, thanking contributors for their support. Emma had seen pictures of the senator and his wife of course, but they seemed so much larger than life in person. Mr. Davidson was every bit as tall and even handsome as his son while his wife looked positively regal.

Emma glanced around the room realizing there were hundreds of people just like them, dressed to the nines, putting on a show of wealth and power meant to impress. No wonder Jaxson had left home at an early age and didn't want to return. If these were the people he'd been surrounded by throughout his childhood, no wonder he appreciated the real relationship he had with her and Chase.

They were almost to the front of the line, ready to be introduced when Jaxson leaned in to whisper to her, "Last chance. Do you want to leave?"

She hugged him closer, going on tiptoe to whisper in his ear, "Where you go, we all go."

She swore she saw tears in his eyes as he whispered back, "Christ, I love you."

Absolutely nothing that happened that night could possibly ruin the joy she felt in that moment, surrounded by the love of not one, but the two men whom she adored.

CHAPTER 20

"*F*ather, Mother, I'd like to introduce you to Emma Fischer, and of course, you remember Chase."

The smile on the senior Mr. Davidson's face never wavered as he leaned in to shake his son's hand and speak into his ear. "I thought we agreed you'd be coming without your hanger-on crowd tonight." The tone of his voice was like ice.

Jaxson felt Emma flinch as if she'd been physically hurt by his father's words. Jaxson watched as she reflexively reached out to link her free arm through Chase's arm to show her support for their lover. God, he was so proud of her for not shrinking with fear before the asshole that was his father.

He kept his cool. "I assumed you'd want as much free publicity as possible, Father. Having Chase here to endorse you is a coup, not to mention, the paparazzi is used to seeing us together."

"That's the damn problem," he groused. "You two need to stop being joined at the hip. There are rumors all over town that you two are queer, doing all kinds of unnatural things. I can't have false accusations flying around. Having Emma with you was going to put those rumors to bed." He glanced sideways, "I'm sure you understand, Chase. Perhaps you can say you've developed a headache and need to leave."

God how Jaxson hated this man, yet he knew he needed to restrain himself. This wasn't the time for this discussion.

Chase didn't seem bothered in the least, reminding Jaxson of what a talented actor his best friend was when he needed to be. "Oh, I certainly do understand, Mr. Davidson. I was just excited to come and help kick your candidacy off with a bang. I'm sure I can dance with a few supporter's wives... maybe have my picture taken with a few babies... you know. Anything for the cause to help draw attention to your candidacy."

Jaxson shot a look at Chase to cool it. He was pouring it on too thick, yet his father was so conceited, Chase's over-the-top rhetoric went over his head. "Well, thank you Chase. I wish my son would take this opportunity as seriously as you are."

His mother stepped forward, anxious to greet her son. "Enough hogging Jaxson, Gregory. I'd like a kiss from both of these handsome young men."

Ever the reserved politician's wife, his mother's version of a public motherly kiss was a small French peck on each of his cheeks, her lips barely touching his skin.

After her kisses to Chase, she turned to Emma. It was only then that he noticed a crack in his mother's solid veneer. He detected tears in her eyes as she smiled the biggest smile he could remember her delivering. "You can't know how very happy I am to meet you, Emma. I've been waiting a long time for this son of mine to finish sewing his wild oats and settle down. I'm hoping you can convince him to move back home where I can maybe see him more than once a year."

Emma hesitated, unsure how to answer his mother's plea. He was about to rescue her when she replied, "I'm not so sure he's ready to settle down just yet since we leave for London tomorrow, but my parents are hoping we'll be spending time stateside as well.

For now, I'm excited to see the world and spend as much time with him and Chase as I can."

Jaxson noted his mother clung to Emma's hands as if she needed the physical touch to believe she was actually there.

"You're adorable. Your eyes are beautiful and your smile... well... I can see what my son sees in you. I want to thank you. When I saw him yesterday, he looked happier, more relaxed, than I ever remember seeing him. I'm pretty sure you have something to do with that."

Emma blushed at his mother's unexpected praise, sneaking a quick glance up at him.

Of course his father had to ruin the moment. "Enough of the family reunion. We need to be mingling with paying guests. Bonnie will let you know when it's time to go on stage for the big announcement."

And just like that they were dismissed, which suited Jaxson just fine. "I'll see you later, Mother."

The three of them followed Bonnie deeper into the ballroom, weaving their way through tables of women in designer gowns and men in expensive tuxedos. Top-shelf champagne flowed freely as waiters mingled passing out caviar and oyster appetizers. The opulence turned Jaxson's stomach as he realized they could feed the homeless in the capital city for a year on the money being dumped on this one event.

He grabbed three flutes of champagne from a passing waiter as soon as they arrived at their assigned table. They were only a few tables from the front of the room, just to the stage left.

All thoughts of attempting to fade into the background were lost when Bonnie steered over several photographers and journalists. He could tell they were attached to his father's campaign. Jaxson tried to keep them away from Chase and Emma, but was unsuccessful. The fact that Jaxson had never brought a date to one of his father's events in the past was working against him. The press smelled blood in the water, knowing Emma had to be someone important to be on his arm. Little did they know that Chase was just as important to Jaxson.

Thankfully, they'd arrived late enough that they didn't have to wait long for dinner to be announced. They settled into their table to eat, grateful Bonnie and two other couples who were high on his father's election committee were at their table and not his parents. The least amount of time they spent in his father's presence the better.

The closer they came to the big announcement, the deeper Jaxson's doubts became. He'd come with a plan, but now that they were here, he wasn't sure he could go through with it. He should have insisted on Chase and Emma staying at the loft.

His parents were making the rounds, greeting each table personally as they made their way to the stage. With each step they took closer to Jaxson's table, the tighter his stress wound.

"Jaxson." Of course Chase noticed. His heart raced. Could he follow-through on his plan? He couldn't bear to look into Chase's eyes.

Chase reached across Emma's lap between them to grasp his hand. The reassuring squeeze brought tears to his eyes. He lifted his napkin to swish the damn things away before a reporter snapped a picture.

Chase leaned in to whisper across Emma, "It's okay, baby. I understand. He's your father."

"I don't understand. Why can't I do it?" Jaxson's doubts surprised himself.

Emma leaned against him, linking her hand silently with the two men. Despite the huge ballroom crowd, his lovers had succeeded in grounding him. In reminding him that he wasn't alone. He would never be alone again.

His heart raced as he weighed the options ahead of him. There had always only been a fifty-fifty chance he'd go through with his plan for the night.

Chase reassured him, signaling he understood Jax well. "If it was just him, you'd drop him in a cold second. But you don't want to hurt your mom. She has to live with him."

As always, Chase knew him better than he knew himself.

Had his father bypassed their table on the way to the podium the night would have ended very differently. Maybe it was fate that made his father stop. Maybe just dumb luck.

His father approached their table, leaning in to talk with the election staffers next to Jax, his angry voice carrying. "I thought I told you not to allow any damn terrorists in tonight. There is a whole table of fucking towel-heads back there sitting next to a table of damn fags who have the nerve to hold hands in public. Do *not* let this happen again, got it?"

His father didn't give his paid staffer a chance to answer. He straightened, putting a fake smile back on his face before announcing to them all that it was time to go to the stage. "It's time the next president makes his candidacy official."

Jaxson's stomach rolled, the expensive food they'd eaten falling like lead into the pit of his gut. Emma was squeezing his hand under the table so hard it now hurt.

He was her Dom. Chase's Dom. He needed to make a decision that would be best not only for the people of the USA, but more importantly for the two people he loved more than anything else in the entire world. They'd pledged their support for whatever decision he made. Could he put them in danger, making them a national target?

One look at Chase's calm face and Jaxson had his answer. He may be their Dom, but he was also their lover. They loved him. They were in this together.

Bonnie and the staffers had already stood and were waiting impatiently for him to join them.

Jaxson pushed to his feet, nodding to Chase before pulling Emma up as well. He wrapped his arm around her protectively as they fell in line behind his parents and the other staffers that were climbing the stairs to the stage where dozens of red, white and blue balloons and flags decorated the space.

Jaxson didn't need to glance backwards to know that Chase was following them onto the stage. They would stand back far enough that his father would hopefully be in the middle of his speech before he realized Chase had joined them.

Bonnie was still too distracted by his father's outburst to be paying any attention. He almost felt sorry for her having to work so closely with his father, yet she did it by choice. She was talented. She could have found a job with any number of other political figures. In fact, he suspected she would need to do just that after tonight.

He forced himself to listen to the condescending and offensive rhetoric spewing from his father's mouth. Never did the man share a positive idea or a kind word about his constituents. His father's entire speech was meant to divide people, pitting poor against rich, white against black, and oppress any demographic that wasn't exactly like his father — rich... white... privileged.

Jaxson felt light headed as his father got to the heart of his platform, spewing hate against immigrants, blacks, gays, lesbians, Muslims, even the poor who took advantage of government aid. That he had to stand on the same stage and even be associated loosely with this man galled him. He couldn't take it anymore.

Jax turned pleading eyes at Chase who smiled, adding a supportive nod.

"And I couldn't have considered taking this historic step if it weren't for the support of my loving family. My wife, Miranda, and son Jaxson along with his girlfriend, Emma Fischer." It was only then his dad glanced behind where Jax stood and saw Chase standing on the other side of Emma.

The time had come. The room was quiet as his father's speech stalled. All eyes were on them as his father shot daggers at his son for allowing Chase to be on the stage with them.

Jaxson turned to Emma then, pulling her into an embrace before capturing her lips in a heated kiss. The second he released her, Chase was there to turn her towards him, hugging her close and planting an even hotter kiss on her open lips. There would be absolutely no misunderstanding by anyone witnessing their passion.

As his lovers broke from their kiss, his father left the podium, stalking towards them in anger. For a second Jaxson thought his father might punch him right then and there. Perhaps that would have turned out better for the senator.

"You sonofabitch, you just couldn't follow-through with your promise. I asked for only one fucking night to get some press from my family." His voice was low, but in his anger it carried far enough that Jaxson could hear the shocked exclamations at the tables close enough to hear the candidate's cussing.

Jaxson stepped closer to his father, their chests almost bumping. "What's the matter, Dad? You asked for me to help you get the national media's attention. Didn't that make a big enough splash for you? If you hated watching Chase and Emma kiss, you're really gonna hate this."

Jaxson stepped back, his knees weak under the stress of the moment. His lover was there to catch him in his arms. They embraced for a few seconds before Chase took control, pulling Jaxson into an open mouth lover's kiss.

Emma snuggled closer, reaching out to hug both men, making it clear she was not with one, but both of them as the three lovers embraced. The room erupted with shouts, boos and even a few rounds of applause just before his father's fist connected with his jaw, ripping Jaxson apart from Chase.

The secret service rushed forward, stepping between the father and son, preventing further punches from being thrown. The room was in pandemonium. It was time for them to leave. His work here was done. Well, almost.

Jaxson pulled apart from his lovers long enough to step closer to his father. He would get the last word. "You asked for my help in getting attention for your national campaign. I just did you a huge favor. I'm certain that my lovers and I just landed you on the front page of every newspaper in the country, hell maybe even the world. You'll be the lead off story for every newscast. Talk shows will be dedicating full episodes to your campaign for days." He went for broke. "Hell, I bet even Juan will see it down in Mexico. No need to thank me, Dad. I'm happy I could help."

Jaxson didn't stay to see the remaining fallout. He didn't need to. He knew he'd just put the final nail into the coffin of his father's burgeoning election campaign. While he was sorry his mother would also be hurt by the fallout as his father's political career disintegrated, he couldn't bring himself to do more than pity her. He'd wait a few days before calling and inviting her to get away from it all in Europe.

They had just hit backstage when a crowd of reporters pressed in, thrusting microphones in their faces, pushing and shoving to get a statement. It was Jaxson they wanted so he released Emma's hand, yelling to Chase to get her safely to the limo and he'd meet them back at the loft.

He watched as his lovers stopped dead in their tracks, turning and fighting to get back to his side. They each held one of his hands and together they started moving again towards the back door where their limo awaited.

"Seriously, you two should go on ahead. I'll catch up."

Emma and Chase grinned up at him and answered in unison, "Where you go, we all go."

THE END

AFTERWORD

Did you enjoy Jaxson, Chase and Emma's story? It doesn't end here. Coming in December 2016, they will be opening a trendy dance club called Runway in the heart of the Georgetown district of Washington DC. Join them for opening night when their friend and rocker, Cash Carter, opens the club with a bang up show. The excitement won't really begin until they all hit the secret, underground BDSM club tucked away in the basement. Black Light is the safe haven for the world's rich and famous to get their most taboo kink on without fear of exposure.

Please enjoy the following excerpt from book one in the series: *Black Light: Rocked*

* * *

The familiar strain of the Crushing Stone's number one hit, *Proving You Wrong,* filled the crowded venue. The rather stuffy crowd that had just minutes before been sipping champagne in their evening wear seemed to shed their restraint to push to their feet as the curtain opened to expose the band to the cheering crowd.

Samantha had to resist the urge to follow several groups of scantily clad women who pressed past her to rush the runway jutting out into the dance floor. Within minutes the stage was surrounded, several layers deep, with raging fans jumping and shouting for the missing lead singer who had yet to grace the show.

Her heart raced, anxious for her first glimpse of Jonah and dreading it at the same time. The second he burst out from back stage the spotlight shone on him, making him the center of attention. She had thought she was prepared, but in that moment Sam found herself fighting down the urge to cry.

What a fool she'd been. She'd come to get a glimpse of her old friend, Jonah, but one glance at the man center stage and Samantha knew she was too late. Jonah was gone, swallowed wholly and completely by his larger-than-life persona, Cash Carter.

And he was devastatingly perfect.

While the room clapped and sang along with the Grammy Award winning band, Samantha sat frozen in the shadows on her tall stool. She couldn't take her eyes off the six-foot tall celebrity currently working the crowd with his sexy dance moves.

She struggled to reconcile the current version of the popular musician with the young man she'd felt so close to most of her life. His signature gravelly voice was deeper than she remembered. God, he'd filled out so much and in all the right places, flexing his muscular arms as he fist pumped to the beat of the angry song. His perfect body was encased in body-hugging black leather pants and a sleeveless shirt. Tattoos rippled across his biceps and his shoulder-length dark hair swayed as he moved with the beat of the song. It was when he moved out onto the long runway, getting closer and closer, that Samantha decided she'd got what she came for after all.

Closure.

Her Jonah was gone.

The reality almost crushed her. It was hard to catch her breath and it was in that moment she had to admit the ugly truth to herself. She'd really come with the hope of feeling a spark of their old connection. That invisible thread that had always bonded them together. Even as young kids, she'd felt connected to Jonah in a way that felt a bit like magic. She'd felt his presence before he became visible. He'd been able to read her mind, understanding her at times better than she understood herself.

The urge to cry was almost too much. Sam swallowed hard, trying to press down the lump in her throat. As the rest of the huge club pressed in around her, she'd never felt as alone as she did watching Jonah reaching down to accept flowers and small gifts from his adoring fans, making tangible connections with strangers he now cared more about than he did her.

He was so close.

An irrational thought took hold. What might he do if she approached the runway? What could she offer him as her gift? She'd already given him her heart and he'd trampled it.

Her fingers flew to the golden heart locket she'd worn around her neck every day since the day he'd given it to her. It had been the day he'd asked her to his senior prom. The day he'd literally swept her off her feet, kissing her until she'd been out of breath. He'd told her it was to be their promise charm to each other. How many nights had she fallen asleep holding that small locket, filled with a lock of his thick hair, feeling closer, if just for minute, to her lost friend?

He won't remember you. He's moved on. And even if he does recognize you, he couldn't care less about you now.

Insanity. Tears finally fell as she sat frozen to her spot, unable to move. She should leave, but instead she felt trapped, there to witness Jonah in all of his perfection as he gyrated his sexy hips like the consummate showman he'd become. She could barely make out the lyrics to the next song, *Betrayal,* for all the screaming fans. It didn't matter. She had every note, every syllable, every melody memorized.

By the time the song was winding down, Samantha knew she had to leave. Instead of feeling better, being so close to Jonah had her on the verge of a full-out panic attack, something she hadn't suffered for years. She was glad now that she hadn't gone too far into the club. She pushed to her wobbly feet, anxious to get outside to the frigid December air in hopes it would revive her.

She crossed in front of several tables of VIPs and patrons sporting press passes. She'd have to weave through a screaming crowd of fans to make it to the exit. The pounding music started to be drowned out by the pounding in her ears as she grew more and more light headed. Panic and the compressed space were closing in faster than she could escape.

The music grew softer, almost subdued. Sam glanced back towards the stage as the band began to play their one and only number one ballad from the year before. The lights that had been trained only on Jonah and the band were now scanning the crowd in a haphazard way as the first chords of *Forever* began, only bringing her tears harder. She'd always hoped he'd been thinking of her as he'd penned the lyrics so now, seeing him walking out onto the runway to touch the dozens of screaming women as the love poured out of him—well it made her feel foolish.

So foolish she was paralyzed as she stood grounded at the end of the runway as Jonah made his way closer with each step he took. Twenty feet. Ten feet.

What she'd give to touch him again, just once. She was as bad as the screaming fans, desperate for any scrap of the famous musician's attention and it made her sick to her stomach to admit how much she'd let his desertion hurt her. He'd never hidden his dreams of being a star from her. She had no right to feel the red-hot anger bubbling up. A true friend would be happy for his success. The fact that she resented having lost Jonah to his Cash Carter guise only made her feel guilty.

He was a mere half-dozen feet away from her now as she stood frozen. Unable to go to him. Unable to leave.

She'd never know if it was fate or weird luck that trained the spotlight from above directly on her. It lasted only for a second, but in that moment he turned her way and their eyes met. His eyes widened slightly as his brow furrowed with surprise. Her brain shouted at her to turn and run away before he shunned her publicly, completing her heartbreaking humiliation, but her feet stood planted in her fashion boots.

How much time passed, she'd never know. What she did know was that the crowd was yelling and the musicians were playing the accompaniment to the song Jonah had stopped singing. Groupies pressed closer to the frozen singer, touching his stationary boots while his glare penetrated her to her core.

He sees me. Really sees me.

The thought thrilled and frightened her. She held her breath until she was light headed. She was in uncharted territory, unsure if she should turn and retreat or advance on the stage. The roving spotlight was back on her, throwing her into the middle of the show whether she liked it or not. She felt all eyes in the three-story club on her as everyone in the room collectively tried to figure out why the` lead singer had suddenly stopped singing one of his most popular songs as if he'd forgotten the lyrics he'd written.

She never took her eyes off his, waiting for his expression to give her a hint of what he was thinking, hopeful she'd see her old Jonah crawl out from behind Cash's polished exterior. She might have been able to handle a nonchalant brush off, but with each second that passed, an angry hatred changed the handsome musician into a frightening adversary.

That's when she realized there had been one outcome she hadn't even considered.

He sees me... and he cares, alright.

He hates me.

ABOUT THE AUTHOR

USA Today bestselling author Livia Grant lives in Chicago with her husband and two sons... one a teenager, the other a furry rescue dog named Max. She is blessed to have traveled extensively and as much as she loves to visit places around the globe, the Midwest and its changing seasons will always be home. Livia started writing when she felt like she finally had the life experience to write a riveting story that she hopes her readers won't be able to put down. Livia's fans appreciate her deep character driven plots, often rooted in an ensemble cast where the friendships are as important as the romance... well, almost. She writes one hell of an erotic romance.

* * *

Connect with Livia!
www.liviagrant.com
lb.grant@yahoo.com

The More the Merrier Two

A Lovely Meal

Sting of Lust

Hero to Obey

Stand Alone Books

Blessed Betrayal

Call Sign: Thunder

THANK YOU FROM LIVIA

Like most authors, I love to hear from my readers. The art of writing can be a lonely activity at times. Authors sit alone, pouring our hearts into our stories, hoping readers will connect with our words and fall in love with our characters. It's easy to get discouraged at times.

And that's where you come in.

I'd sure appreciate it if you'd take a few minutes to drop me a line or better yet, leave a review to let me know what you thought of the book you just finished. Reader feedback, good and bad, is what helps me continue to grow stronger as an author.

Happy reading!
Livia

Made in the USA
Columbia, SC
20 December 2019

85450372R00126